Price Guide to Big Little Books

& Better Little, Jumbo, Tiny Tales, A Fast-Action Story etc.

© 1995

L-W BOOK SALES
P.O. Box 69
Gas City, IN 46933

ISBN#: 0-89538-041-2

Copyright 1995 by
L-W Book Sales

All rights reserved. No part of this work may be reproduced
or used in any forms or by any means – graphic, electronic, or
mechanical, including photocopying or storage and retrieval
systems – without written permission from the copyright holder.

Published By: L-W Book Sales
P.O. Box 69
Gas City, IN 46933

Printed by IMAGE GRAPHICS, INC., Paducah, Kentucky

Please write for our free catalog.

TABLE OF CONTENTS

Big Little Books/Better Little Books 4-55, 64-68, 71-72

Big Little Nickel Book (1 shown) 5

Whitman 56-59

Tiny Tales 60-61

New Little Better Books 62-63

A Top-Line Comic 64

Radio Play Script 64

Miscellaneous 69

The Big Little Book TV Series 70

A Fast-Action Story, Dell 73-77

Saalfield Books 77-93

A Lynn Books 94-96

Engle Van-Wiseman 96-98

Famous Comics 99

The World Syndicate Publishing Co. 100

Samuel Lowe Co. 101

Golden Press 102-103

All books pictured are shown at 50% of their original size.

INTRODUCTION

With the onset of the twentieth century, paperbound forms of entertainment had reached a new peak of popularity. Volumes of classic literature rolled off the presses, along with an abundance of childrens' tales, daily newspaper editions, school books, pulps and other magazines which were immensely popular at the time. The entertainment field was also burgeoning with other media, including motion pictures, live theater, and radio show performances.

Youngsters of all ages would scrimp and save their hard-earned allowances for the true necessities of life: candy, a toy, a carnival ticket, and a good book (a truly foreign notion to the adolescents of today, bred on Saturday morning cartoons interspersed with a few hours of video games). Juvenile boys of the era beheld such fictional idols as Buck Rogers, Tom Mix, and Dan Dunn, while young maidens of the day preferred to read about heroic starlets such as Peggy Brown, Brenda Starr, and Little Orphan Annie. The theater was only an occasional treat, therefore reading was instrumental to the flourishing daydreams of millions of youth.

In 1933, Whitman Publishing Co. of Racine, Wisconsin, began to provide the first Big Little Book to the public, of which *Dick Tracy* was the featured story. A previous history of producing fairy tales and boy adventure stories throughout the twenties, Whitman presented the notion of Big Little Books – just the right size for young readers containing the stories these readers wanted. A tremendous hit at the time, Big Little Books expanded their sales line to include many forms of fictional heroes, classic literature, cartoon characters, and characters and events borrowed from motion pictures, radio, and later, the television set. Kids of all ages could peruse across pages of story with eye-catching pictures throughout and pass away the day immersed in terrific tales of danger, exciting cliffhangers, dramatic character relations, and even gutbusting fun fables of the best the funny pages had to offer.

Whitman began a trend soon to be followed by other publishers such as Saalfield, Goldsmith, Lynn, and Dell Publishing Co. While entering their own books into the fray (along with similar size and format), they could not topple Whitman from the top of the list. Big Little Books continued to publish and reprint titles clear into the early 1970's. During this time, Big Little Books did acquire stiff competition from comic book companies, who began amassing popularity by introducing completely new stories and characters, while at the same time utilizing other popular characters and storylines of the period. Oddly enough, it was a year after Big Little Books' first release when comic book fandom began in full swing, becoming a tremendous market unto itself which still thrives to this very day. During later years, Whitman Publishing benefited from these comic book characters when their favorite characters found a new residence nestled within the pages of a Big Little Book.

The relentless search for Big Little Books continues to propel thousands of collectors throughout antique paper periodicals, collector's malls, flea markets, garage sales, and antique dealer events. The colorful covers bound onto pocket sized tomes attract crowds from all sorts of collectible fields – from paper collectors to comic interest, all may find a place in their heart for Big Little Books.

PRICING NOTE

The current values in this book should be used only as a guide. They are not intended to set prices, which vary from one section of the country to another. Auction prices as well as dealer prices vary greatly and are affected by condition as well as demand. The publisher nor the contributors assumes responsibility for any losses or gains that might be incurred as a result of consulting this guide.

BIG LITTLE BOOKS / BETTER LITTLE BOOKS
Whitman

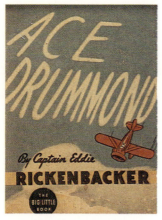

Ace Drummond,
© 1935, book #1177.
$15

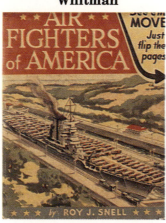

Air Fighters of America,
© 1941, book #1448.
$30

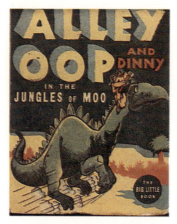

Alley Oop and Dinny
in the Jungles of Moo
© 1938, book #1473.
$35

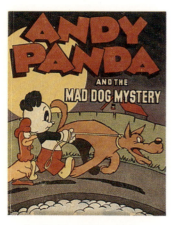

Andy Panda and the
Mad Dog Mystery
© 1947, book #1431.
$20

Andy Panda's Vacation
© 1946, book #1485.
$25

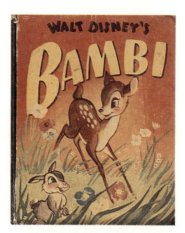

Bambi, Walt Disney's
© 1942, book #1469.
$30

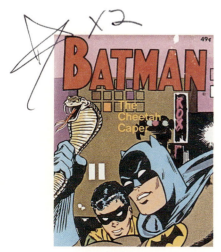

Batman
The Cheetah Caper
© 1969, book #5771.
$10

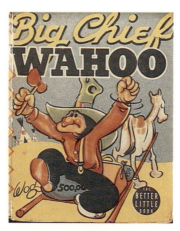

Big Chief Wahoo
© 1938, book #1443.
$25

Black Silver
Pirate Crew
© 1937, book #1414.
$20

5

BIG LITTLE BOOKS / BETTER LITTLE BOOKS
Whitman

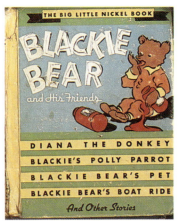

Blackie Bear and His
Friends, (Big Little
Nickel Book)
© 1935, book #1005.
$15

Blaze Brandon with the
Foreign Legion
© 1938, book #1447.
$25

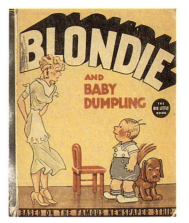

Blondie and Baby
Dumpling
© 1937, book #1415.
$40

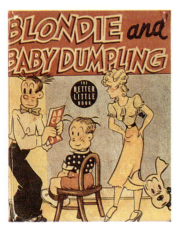

Blondie and Baby
Dumpling
© 1939, book #1429.
$30

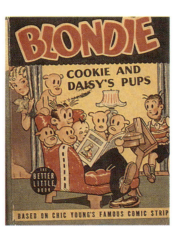

Blondie Cookie and
Daisy's Pups
© 1943, book #1491.
$20

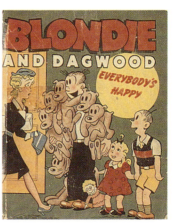

Blondie and Dagwood
Everybody's Happy
© 1948, book #1438.
$25

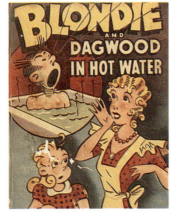

Blondie and Dagwood
in Hot Water
© 1946, book #1410.
$30

Blondie
Papa Knows Best
© 1945, book #1490.
$15

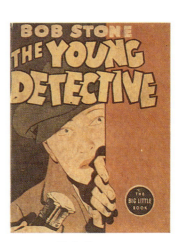

Bob Stone
The Young Detective
© 1937, book #1432.
$20

BIG LITTLE BOOKS / BETTER LITTLE BOOKS
Whitman

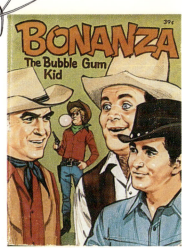

Bonanza
The Bubble Gum Kid
© 1967, book #2002.
$15

Brad Turner in
Transatlantic Flight
© 1939, book #1425.
$30

Brenda Starr and the
Masked Impostor
© 1943, book #1427.
$35

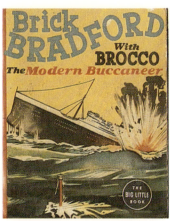

Brick Bradford with Brocco
The Modern Buccaneer
© 1938, book #1468.
$15

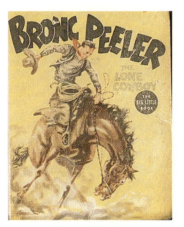

Bronc Peeler
The Lone Cowboy
© 1937, book #1417.
$10

The Buccaneer
© 1938, book #1470.
$30

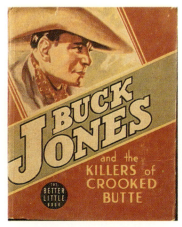

Buck Jones and the
Killers of Crooked Butte
© 1940, book #1451.
$40

Buck Jones in the
Roaring West
© 1935, book #1174.
$25

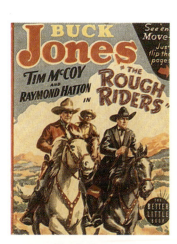

Buck Jones
The Rough Riders
© 1943, book #1486.
$40

BIG LITTLE BOOKS / BETTER LITTLE BOOKS
Whitman

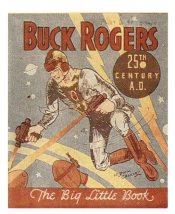

Buck Rogers
25th Century A.D.
© 1933, no book number,
paperback.
$100

Buck Rogers
25th Century A.D.
© 1933, book #742.
$100

Buck Rogers in the City
of Floating Globes
© 1935, giveaway.
$150

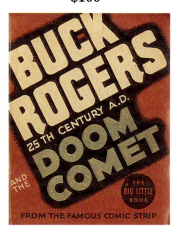

Buck Rogers 25th
Century A.D.
Doom Comet
© 1935, book #1178.
$75

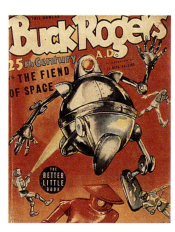

Buck Rogers 25th
Century A.D. vs The
Fiend of Space
© 1940, book #1409.
$75

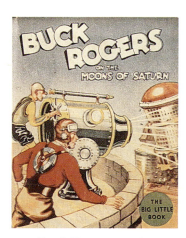

Buck Rogers on the
Moons of Saturn
© 1934, book #1143.
$50

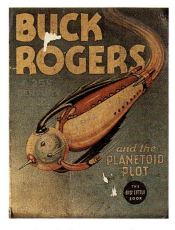

Buck Rogers 25th
Century A.D. and the
Planetoid Plot
© 1936, book #1197.
$90

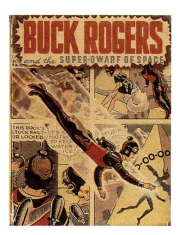

Buck Rogers and the
Super-Dwarf of Space
© 1943, book #1490.
$55

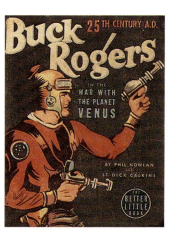

Buck Rogers 25th
Century A.D. in the War
With The Planet Venus
© 1938, book #1437.
$50

BIG LITTLE BOOKS / BETTER LITTLE BOOKS
Whitman

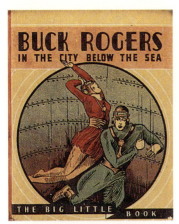

Buck Rogers in the
City Below The Sea
© 1934, book #765.
$40

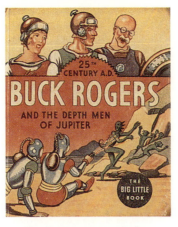

Buck Rogers and the
Depth Men of Jupiter
© 1937, book #1169.
$80

Buffalo Bill Plays
A Lone Hand
© 1936, book #1194.
$15

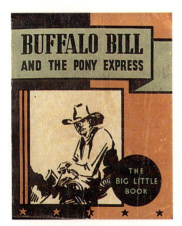

Buffalo Bill and the
Pony Express
© 1934, book #713.
$20

Bugs Bunny and His Pals
© 1945, book #1496.
$50

Bugs Bunny and the
Pirate Loot
© 1945, book #1403.
$30

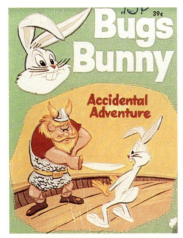

Bugs Bunny
Accidental Adventure
© 1969, book #2029.
$20

Bugs Bunny Accidental
Adventure, (Flip it cartoons)
© 1973, book #5758-1.
$20

Bugs Bunny and
Klondike Gold
© 1948, book #1455.
$25

BIG LITTLE BOOKS / BETTER LITTLE BOOKS
Whitman

Bugs Bunny and Klondike
Gold (Flip-it cartoons).
Reissue of book #1455
book #5766.
$10

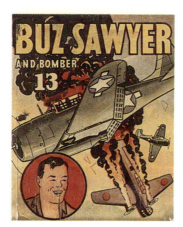

Buz Sawyer and
Bomber 13
© 1946, book #1415.
$20

Calling W-1-X-Y-Z
Jimmy Kean and the
Radio Spies
© 1939, book #1412.
$20

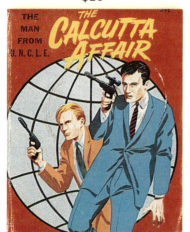

The Calcutta Affair
(The Man from U.N.C.L.E.)
© 1967, book #2011.
$15

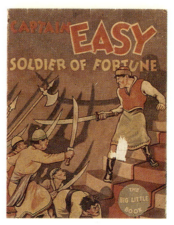

Captain Easy
Soldier of Fortune
© 1934, book #1128.
$25

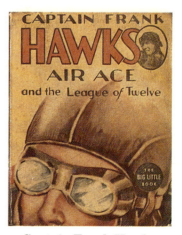

Captain Frank Hawks
Air Ace and the
League of Twelve
© 1938, book #1444.
$15

Captain Midnight and
the Secret Squadron
© 1941, book #1488.
$55

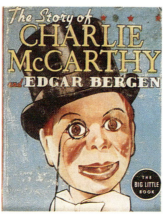

The Story of Charlie
McCarthy & Edgar Bergen
© 1938, book #1456.
$20

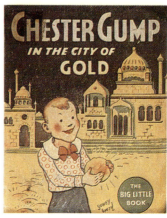

Chester Gump in the
City of Gold
© 1935, book #1146.
$75

BIG LITTLE BOOKS / BETTER LITTLE BOOKS
Whitman

Chester Gump Finds
The Hidden Treasure
© 1934, book #766.
$60

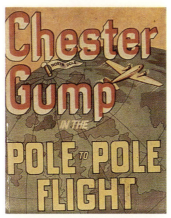

Chester Gump in the
Pole to Pole Flight
© 1937, book #1402.
$25

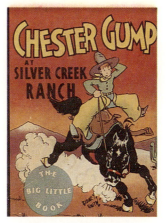

Chester Gump at
Silver Creek Ranch
© 1933, book #734.
$35

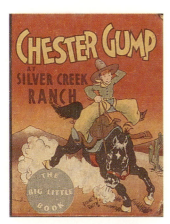

Chester Gump at
Silver Creek Ranch,
book #7 giveaway.
$35

Chitty Chitty
Bang Bang
© 1968, book #2025.
$5

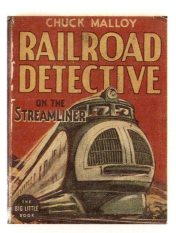

Chuck Malloy Railroad
Detective on the
Streamliner
© 1938, book #1453.
$15

Clyde Beatty Daredevil
Lion and Tiger Tamer
© 1939, book #1410.
$15

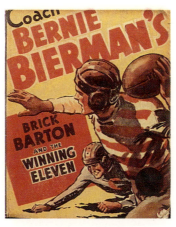

Coach Bernie Bierman's
Brick Barton and the
Winning Eleven
© 1938, book #1480.
$40

Convoy Patrol A Thrilling U.S. Navy Story
© 1942, book #1446.
$40

BIG LITTLE BOOKS / BETTER LITTLE BOOKS
Whitman

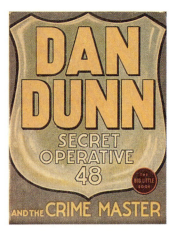

Dan Dunn Secret
Operative 48 and the
Crime Master
© 1937, book #1171.
$20

Dan Dunn Secret
Operative 48 and the
Dope Ring
© 1940, book #1492.
$20

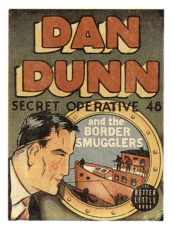

Dan Dunn Secret
Operative 48 and the
Border Smugglers
© 1938, book #1418.
$30

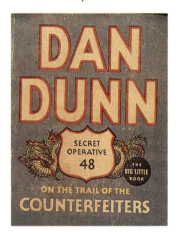

Dan Dunn Secret
Operative 48 on the Trail
of the Counterfeiters
© 1936, book #1125
$20

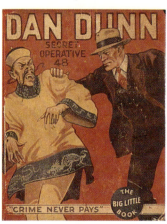

Dan Dunn Secret
Operative 48
Crime Never Pays
© 1934, book #1116.
$20

Dan Dunn Secret
Operative 48 on the
Trail of Wu Fang
© 1938, book #1454.
$15

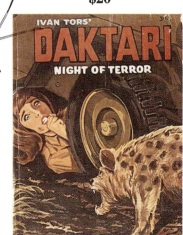

Ivan Tors' Daktari
Night of Terror
© 1968, book #2018.
$5

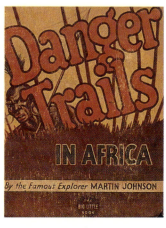

Danger Trails in Africa
© 1935, book #1151.
$20

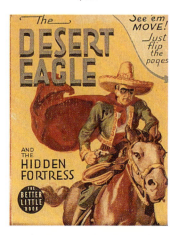

The Desert Eagle and
the Hidden Fortress
© 1941, book #1431.
$25

BIG LITTLE BOOKS / BETTER LITTLE BOOKS
Whitman

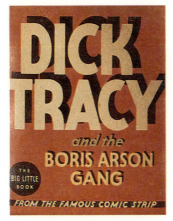

Dick Tracy and the
Boris Arson Gang
© 1935, book #1163.
$35

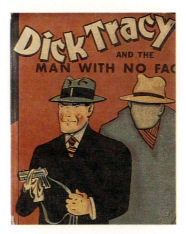

Dick Tracy and the
Man With No Face
© 1938, book #1491.
$40

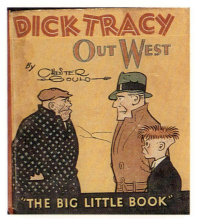

Dick Tracy Out West
© 1933, book #723.
$55

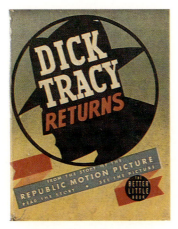

Dick Tracy Returns
© 1939, book #1495.
$35

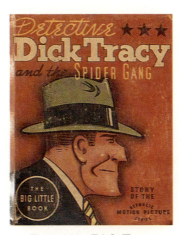

Detective Dick Tracy
and the Spider Gang
© 1937, book #1446.
$35

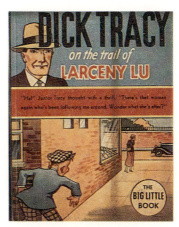

Dick Tracy on the
Trail of Larceny Lu
© 1935, book #1170.
$35

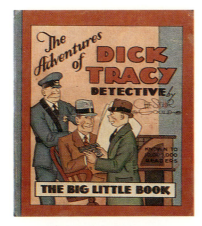

The Adventures of
Dick Tracy Detective
© 1932, book #707.
$90

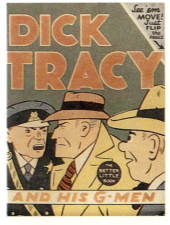

Dick Tracy and His G-Men
© 1941, book #1439.
$35

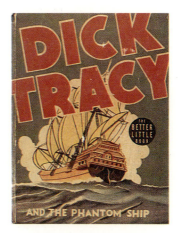

Dick Tracy and the
Phantom Ship
© 1940, book #1434.
$35

BIG LITTLE BOOKS / BETTER LITTLE BOOKS
Whitman

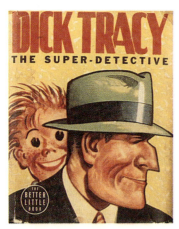

Dick Tracy
the Super-Detective
© 1939, book #1488.
$30

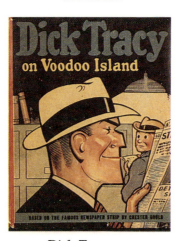

Dick Tracy on
Voodoo Island
© 1944, book #1478.
$45

Dick Tracy and
Yogee Yamma
© 1946, book #1412.
$30

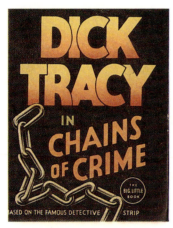

Dick Tracy in
Chains of Crime
© 1936, book #1185.
$35

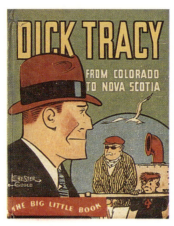

Dick Tracy from
Colorado to Nova Scotia
© 1933, book #749.
$40

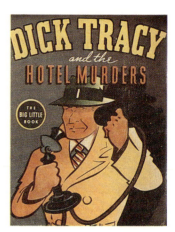

Dick Tracy and the
Hotel Murders
© 1937, book #1420.
$40

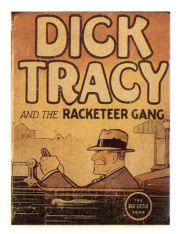

Dick Tracy and the
Racketeer Gang
© 1936, book #1112.
$35

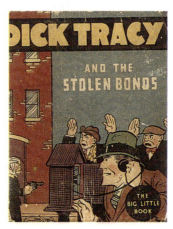

Dick Tracy and the
Stolen Bonds
© 1934, book #1105.
$45

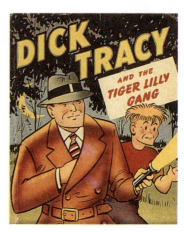

Dick Tracy and the
Tiger Lilly Gang
© 1949, book #1460.
$30

BIG LITTLE BOOKS / BETTER LITTLE BOOKS
Whitman

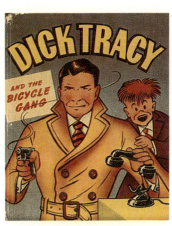

Dick Tracy and the
Bicycle Gang
© 1948, book #1445.
$30

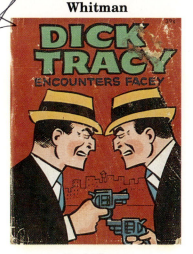

Dick Tracy
Encounters Facey
© 1967, book #2001.
$15

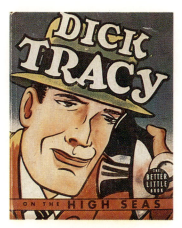

Dick Tracy on the
High Seas
© 1939, book #1454.
$35

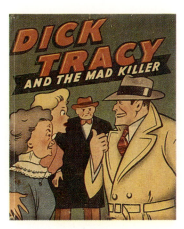

Dick Tracy and the
Mad Killer
© 1947, book #1436.
$40

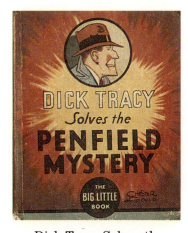

Dick Tracy Solves the
Penfield Mystery
© 1934, book #1137.
$40

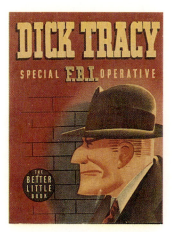

Dick Tracy Special F.B.I.
Operative
© 1943, book #1449.
$35

Don Winslow
and the Giant Girl Spy
© 1946, book #1408.
$20

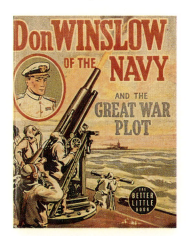

Don Winslow of the Navy
and the Great War Plot
© 1940, book #1489.
$20

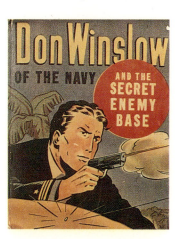

Don Winslow of the Navy
& the Secret Enemy Base
© 1943, book #1453.
$30

BIG LITTLE BOOKS / BETTER LITTLE BOOKS
Whitman

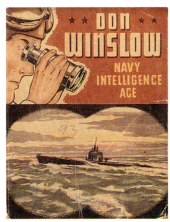

Don Winslow Navy
Intelligence Ace
© 1942, book #1418.
$25

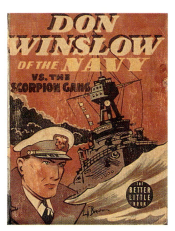

Don Winslow of the Navy
vs. The Scorpion Gang
© 1938, book #419.
$25

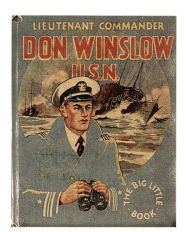

Lieutenant Commander
Don Winslow U.S.N.
© 1935, book #1107.
$40

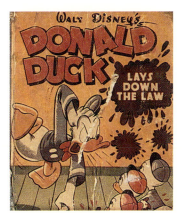

Donald Duck
Lays Down the Law
© 1948, book #1449.
$35

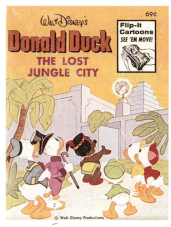

Donald Duck
The Lost Jungle City
© 1975, book #5773.
$5

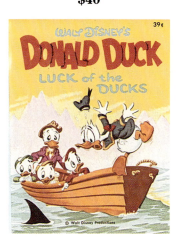

Donald Duck Luck
of the Ducks (soft cover)
© 1969, book #5764.
$10

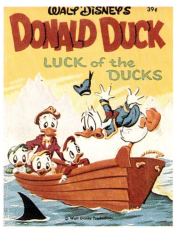

Donald Duck Luck of
the Ducks (hard cover)
© 1969, book #2033.
$15

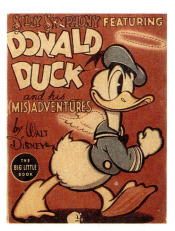

Silly Symphony Featuring
Donald Duck and his
Misadventures
© 1937, book #1441.
$65

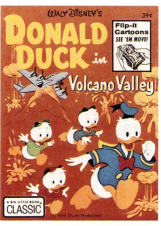

Donald Duck in
Volcano Valley
© 1973, book #5760.
$5

BIG LITTLE BOOKS / BETTER LITTLE BOOKS
Whitman

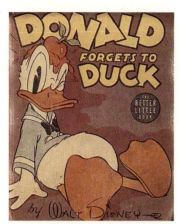

Donald Forgets to Duck
© 1939, book #1434.
$30

Donald Duck
Off The Beam
© 1943, book #1438.
$45

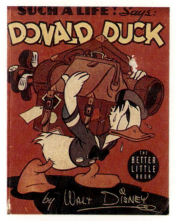

Such A Life! Says:
Donald Duck
© 1939, book #1404.
$30

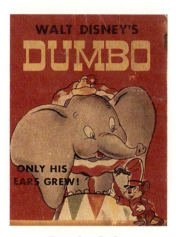

Dumbo Only
His Ears Grew!
© 1941, book #1400.
$50

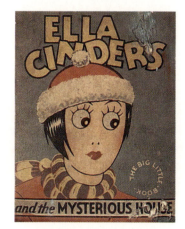

Ella Cinders and the
Mysterious House
© 1934, book #1106.
$45

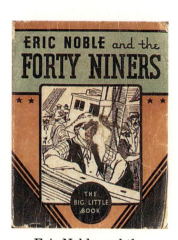

Eric Noble and the
Forty Niners
© 1934, book #772.
$15

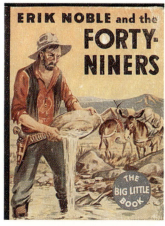

Erik Noble and the
Forty-Niners
© 1934, book #772.
$30

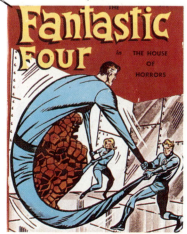

Fantastic Four in the
House of Horrors
© 1968, book #2019.
$10

Flash Gordon and the
Fiery Desert of Mongo
© 1948, book #1447.
$50

BIG LITTLE BOOKS / BETTER LITTLE BOOKS
Whitman

Flash Gordon in the
Forest Kingdom of Mongo
© 1938, book #1492.
$50

Flash Gordon and the
Power Men of Mongo
© 1943, book #1469.
$60

Flash Gordon and the
Red Sword Invaders
© 1945, book #1479.
$55

Flash Gordon in the
Jungles of Mongo
© 1947, book #1424.
$60

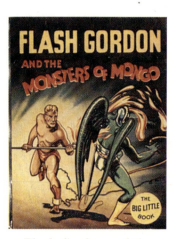

Flash Gordon and the
Monsters of Mongo
© 1935, book #1166.
$70

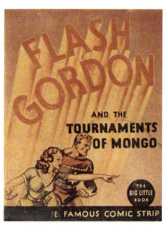

Flash Gordon and the
Tournaments of Mongo
© 1935, book #1171.
$60

Flash Gordon and the
Tyrant of Mongo
© 1941, book #1484.
$70

Flash Gordon and the
Water World of Mongo
© 1937, book #1407.
$65

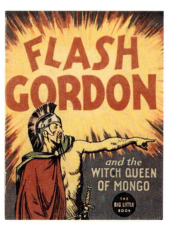

Flash Gordon and the
Witch Queen of Mongo
© 1936, book #1190.
$70

BIG LITTLE BOOKS / BETTER LITTLE BOOKS
Whitman

Flash Gordon in
The Ice World of Mongo
© 1942, book #1443.
$60

Flash Gordon on the
Planet Mongo
© 1934, book #1110.
$80

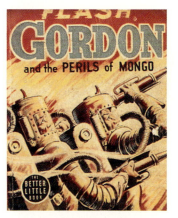

Flash Gordon and the
Pearls of Mongo
© 1940, book #1423.
$60

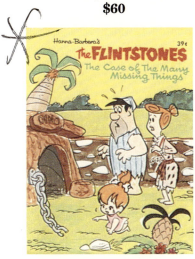

The Flintstones,
The Case of the Many
Missing Things
© 1968, book #2014.
$5

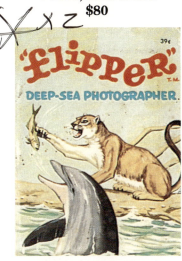

Flipper, Deep-Sea
Photographer
© 1969, book #2032.
$10

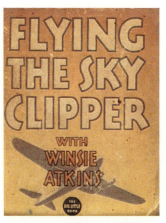

Flying The Sky Clipper
with Winsie Atkins
© 1936, book #1108.
$15

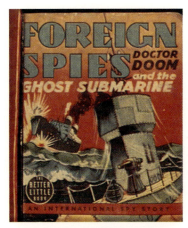

Foreign Spies Doctor Doom
and the Ghost Submarine
© 1939, book #1460.
$35

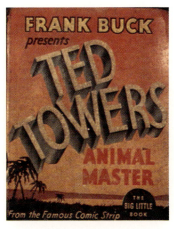

Frank Buck Presents Ted
Towers Animal Master
© 1935, book #1175.
$25

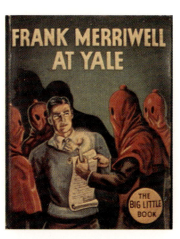

Frank Merriwell At Yale
© 1935, book #1121.
$15

BIG LITTLE BOOKS / BETTER LITTLE BOOKS
Whitman

Frankenstein, Jr. The
Menace of
The Heartless Monster
© 1968, book #2015.
$5

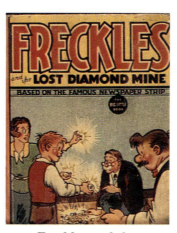

Freckles and the
Lost Diamond Mine
© 1937, book #1164.
$30

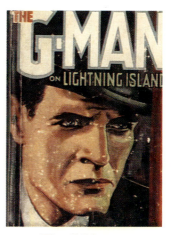

The G-Man on
Lightning Island
© 1936, book #6833.
$30

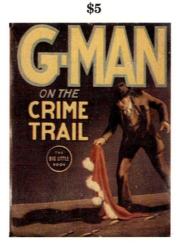

G-Man on the Crime Trail
© 1936, book #1118.
$20

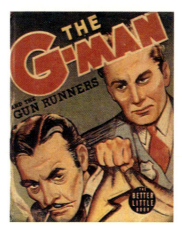

The G-Man and the
Gun Runners
© 1940, book #1469.
$20

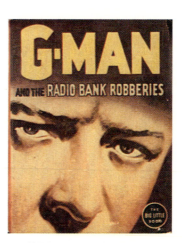

G-Man and the Radio
Bank Robberies
© 1937, book #1434.
$20

G-Man vs.
The Fifth Column
© 1941, book #1470.
$25

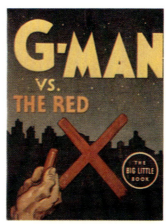

G-Man vs. The Red X
© 1936, book #1147.
$30

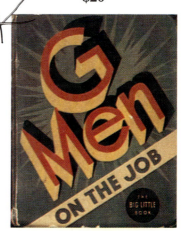

G Men On The Job
© 1935, book #1168.
$20

BIG LITTLE BOOKS / BETTER LITTLE BOOKS
Whitman

Gang Busters in Action
© 1938, book #1451.
$20

Gang Busters
Smash Through
© 1942, book #1437.
$15

Gang Busters Step In
© 1939, book #1433.
$25

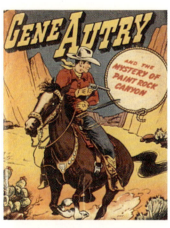

Gene Autry and the
Mystery of
Paint Rock Canyon
© 1946, book #1409.
$25

Gene Autry and Raiders
of the Range
© 1947, book #1425.
$30

Gene Autry and Raiders
of the Range
© 1946, book #1409.
$30

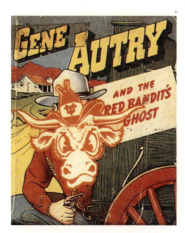

Gene Autry and the Red
Bandit's Ghost
© 1949, book #1461.
$25

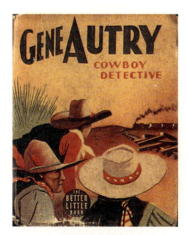

Gene Autry
Cowboy Detective
© 1940, book #1494.
$25

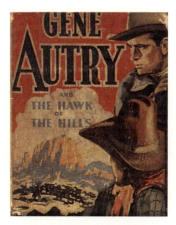

Gene Autry and The
Hawk of The Hills
© 1942, book #1493.
$45

BIG LITTLE BOOKS / BETTER LITTLE BOOKS
Whitman

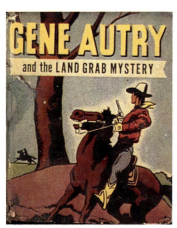

Gene Autry and the
Land Grab Mystery
© 1948, book #1439.
$25

Gentle Ben
© 1969, book #2035.
$5

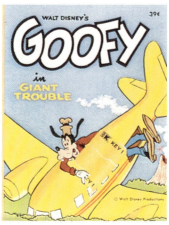

Goofy in Giant Trouble
© 1968, book #5751.
$5

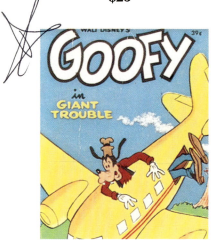

Goofy in Giant Trouble
© 1968, book #2021.
$10

Grimm's Ghost Stories
© 1971, book #5778-1.
$5

Houdini's Magic
© 1927, giveaway.
$30

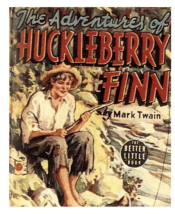

The Adventures of
Huckleberry Finn
© 1939, book #1422.
$20

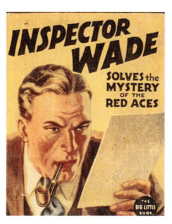

Inspector Wade Solves the
Mystery of the Red Aces
© 1937, book #1448.
$30

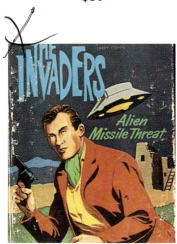

The Invaders Alien
Missile Threat
© 1967, book #2012.
$5

BIG LITTLE BOOKS / BETTER LITTLE BOOKS
Whitman

Invisible Scarlet O'Neil
vs The King of the Slums
© 1946, book #1406.
$20

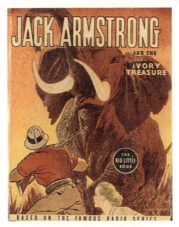

Jack Armstrong and the
Ivory Treasure
© 1937, book #1435.
$25

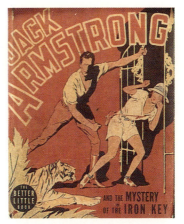

Jack Armstrong and the
Mystery of the Iron Key
© 1939, book #1432.
$25

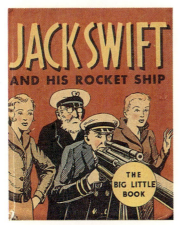

Jack Swift and
His Rocket Ship
© 1934, book #1102.
$30

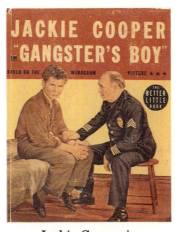

Jackie Cooper in
"Gangster's Boy"
© 1939, book #1402.
$45

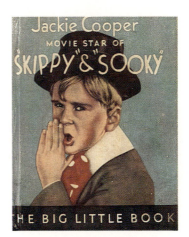

Jackie Cooper Movie
Star of Skippy & Sooky
© 1933, book #714.
$20

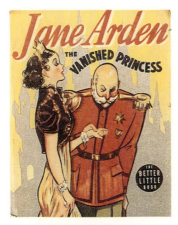

Jane Arden the
Vanished Princess
© 1938, book #1498.
$20

Jane Withers in
Keep Smiling
© 1938, book #1463.
$15

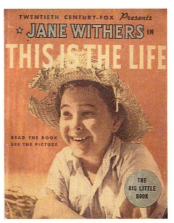

Jane Withers in
This Is The Life
© 1935, book #1179.
$15

BIG LITTLE BOOKS / BETTER LITTLE BOOKS
Whitman

Jim Starr of the
Border Patrol
© 1937, book #1428.
$15

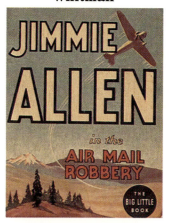

Jimmie Allen in the
Air Mail Robbery
© 1936, book #1143.
$25

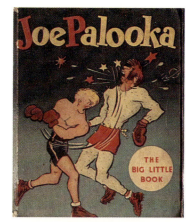

Joe Palooka
© 1934, book #1123.
$25

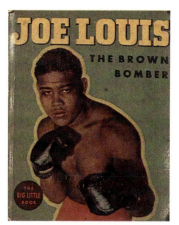

Joe Louis
The Brown Bomber
© 1936, book #1105.
$30

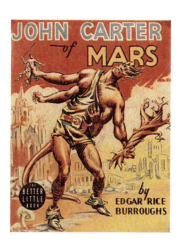

John Carter of Mars
© 1940, book #1402.
$75

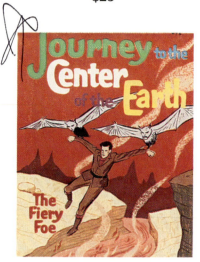

Journey to the Center of
the Earth The Fiery Foe
© 1968, book #2026.
$5

Jungle Jim
© 1936, book #1138.
$40

Jungle Jim and the
Vampire Woman
© 1937, book #1139.
$40

Junior G-Men
© 1937, book #1442.
$30

BIG LITTLE BOOKS / BETTER LITTLE BOOKS
Whitman

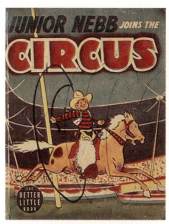

Junior Nebb
Joins The Circus
© 1939, book #1470.
$15

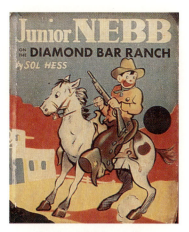

Junior Nebb on the
Diamond Bar Ranch
© 1938, book #1422.
$15

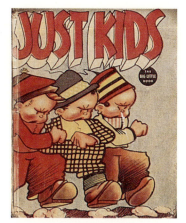

Just Kids
© 1937, book #1401.
$35

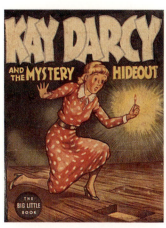

Kay Darcy and the
Mystery Hideout
© 1937, book #1411.
$15

Kayo and Moon Mullins
and the One Man Gang
© 1939, book #1415.
$45

Kazan in Revenge
of the North
The Story of a Great Dog
© 1937, book #1105.
$15

Kazan King of the Pack
© 1940, book #1471.
$20

Ken Maynard and the
Gun Wolves of the Gila
© 1939, book #1442.
$20

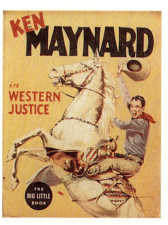

Ken Maynard in
Western Justice
© 1938, book #1430.
$20

BIG LITTLE BOOKS / BETTER LITTLE BOOKS
Whitman

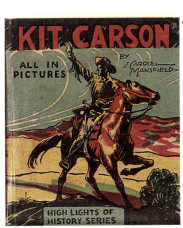

Kit Carson
© 1933.
$15

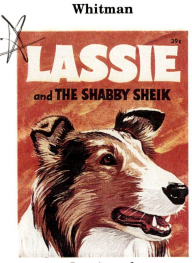

Lassie and
The Shabby Sheik
© 1968, book #2027.
$5

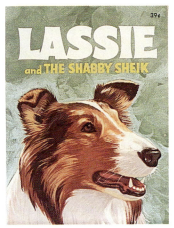

Lassie and
The Shabby Sheik
© 1968, book #5762.
$5

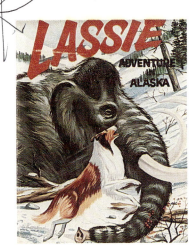

Lassie Adventure
in Alaska
© 1967, book #2004.
$5

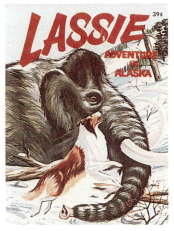

Lassie Adventure
in Alaska
© 1967, book #5754.
$5

The Laughing
Dragon of Oz
© 1934, book #1126.
$75

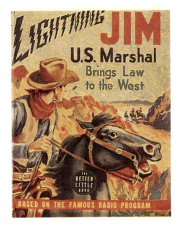

Lightning Jim
U.S. Marshal Brings
Law to the West
© 1940, book #1441.
$15

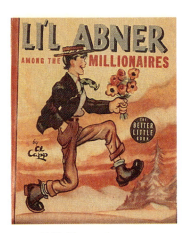

Li'l Abner Among
The Millionaires
© 1939, book #1401.
$40

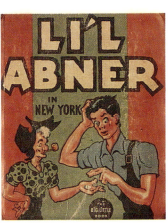

Li'l Abner in New York
© 1936, book #1198.
$40

BIG LITTLE BOOKS / BETTER LITTLE BOOKS
Whitman

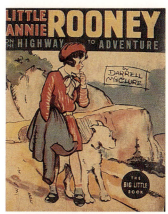

Little Annie Rooney on the
Highway to Adventure
© 1938, book #1406.
$15

Little Annie Rooney and
the Orphan House
© 1936, book #1117.
$25

Little Big Shot
© 1935, book #1149.
$20

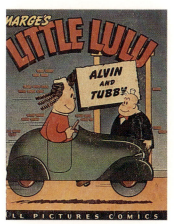

Marge's Little Lulu
Alvin and Tubby
© 1947, book #1429.
$25

Little Miss Muffet
© 1936, book #1120.
$15

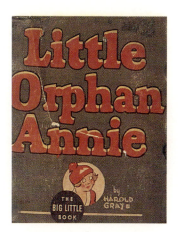

Little Orphan Annie
© 1935, book #1162.
$40

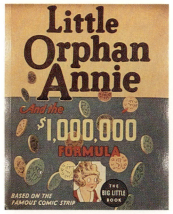

Little Orphan Annie and
the $1,000,000 Formula
© 1936, book #1186.
$35

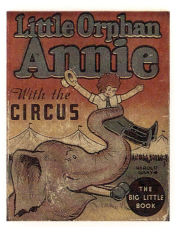

Little Orphan Annie
with the Circus
© 1934, book #1103.
$55

Little Orphan Annie and
the Haunted Mansion
© 1937, book #1482.
$45

BIG LITTLE BOOKS / BETTER LITTLE BOOKS
Whitman

Little Orphan Annie in
the Movies
© 1937, book #1416.
$30

Little Orphan Annie in
the Thieves' Den
© 1948, book #1446.
$30

Little Orphan Annie
and the Underground
Hide-Out
© 1945, book #1461.
$40

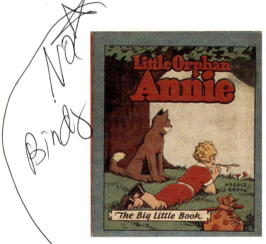

Little Orphan Annie
© 1933, book #708.
$80

Little Orphan Annie and
the Ancient Treasure of Am
© 1939, book #1468.
$40

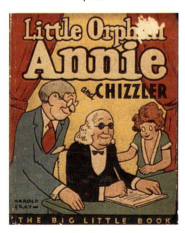

Little Orphan Annie
and Chizzler
© 1933, book #748.
$40

Little Orphan Annie and
the Gooneyville Mystery
© 1947, book #1435.
$30

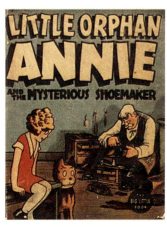

Little Orphan Annie and
the Mysterious Shoemaker
© 1938, book #1449.
$35

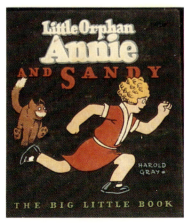

Little Orphan Annie
and Sandy
© 1933, book #716.
$60

BIG LITTLE BOOKS / BETTER LITTLE BOOKS
Whitman

Little Orphan Annie and
the Ancient Treasure of Am
© 1939, book #1414.
$50

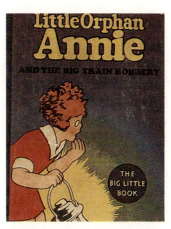
Little Orphan Annie and
the Big Train Robbery
© 1934, book #1140.
$40

Little Orphan Annie and
her Junior Commandos
© 1942, book #1487.
$30

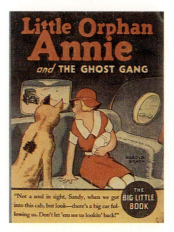
Little Orphan Annie and
the Ghost Gang
© 1935, book #1140.
$40

Little Orphan Annie and
the Secret of the Well
© 1947, book #1417.
$25

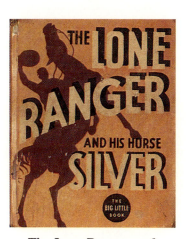
The Lone Ranger and
His Horse Silver
© 1935, book #1181.
$60

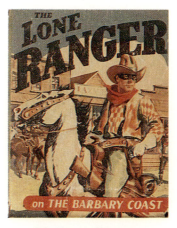
The Lone Ranger
on the Barbary Coast
© 1944, book #1421.
$30

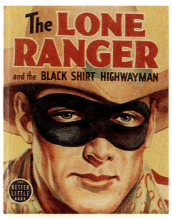
The Lone Ranger and the
Black Shirt Highwayman
© 1939, book #1450.
$40

The Lone Ranger and
Dead Men's Mine
© 1939, book #1407.
$35

BIG LITTLE BOOKS / BETTER LITTLE BOOKS
Whitman

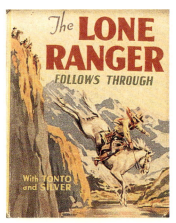

The Lone Ranger Follows Through w/ Tonto and Silver
© 1937, book #1416.
$30

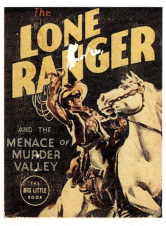

The Lone Ranger and the Menace of Murder Valley
© 1938, book #1465.
$35

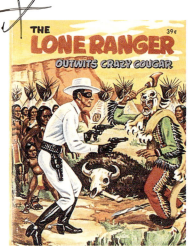

The Lone Ranger Outwits Crazy Cougar
© 1968, book #2013.
$5

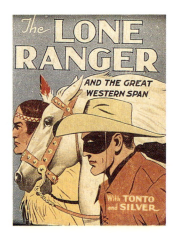

The Lone Ranger and the Great Western Span with Tonto and Silver
© 1939, book #1477.
$40

The Lone Ranger and the Red Renegades
© 1939, book #1489.
$30

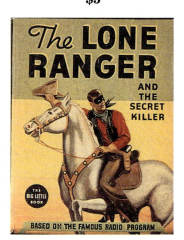

The Lone Ranger and the Secret Killer
© 1937, book #1431.
$40

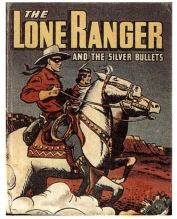

The Lone Ranger and the Silver Bullets
© 1946, book #1498.
$35

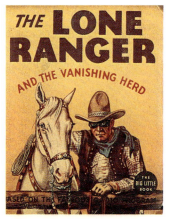

The Lone Ranger and the Vanishing Herd
© 1936, book #1196.
$35

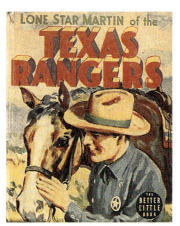

Lone Star Martin of the Texas Rangers
© 1939, book #1405.
$15

BIG LITTLE BOOKS / BETTER LITTLE BOOKS
Whitman

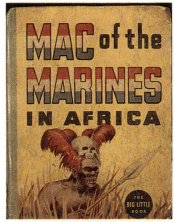

Mac of the Marines
in Africa
© 1936, book #1189.
$25

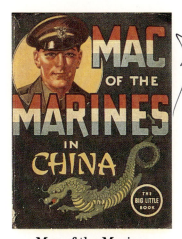

Mac of the Marines
in China
© 1938, book #1400.
$20

Major Matt Mason
Moon Mission
© 1968, book #2022.
$15

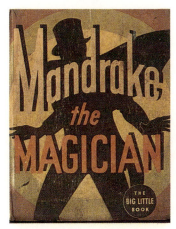

Mandrake the Magician
© 1935, book #1167.
$45

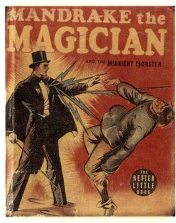

Mandrake the Magician
and the Midnight Monster
© 1939, book #1431.
$30

Mandrake the Magician
Mighty Solver of Mysteries
© 1941, book #1454.
$35

Mandrake The Magician
and the Flame Pearls
© 1942, book #1418.
$40

Mary Lee and the Mystery
of the Indian Beads
© 1937, book #1438.
$15

Master Detective
Ellery Queen, Adventure
of the Murdered Million
© 1942, book #1472.
$20

BIG LITTLE BOOKS / BETTER LITTLE BOOKS
Whitman

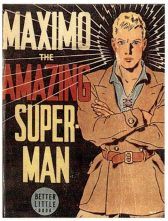
Maximo the Amazing
Superman
© 1940, book #1436.
$25

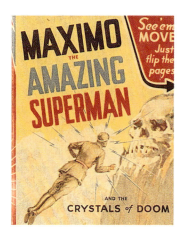
Maximo the Amazing
Superman and the
Chrystals of Doom
© 1941, book #1444.
$25

Maximo the Amazing
Superman and the
Supermachine
© 1941, book #1445.
$25

Men of the Mounted
Adventures of the Canadian
Royal Mounted
© 1934, giveaway.
$30

Men of the Mounted
Adventures of the Canadian
Royal Mounted
© 1934, book #755.
$40

Men with Wings
© 1938, book #1475.
$15

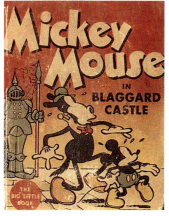
Mickey Mouse in
Blaggard Castle
© 1934, giveaway.
$50

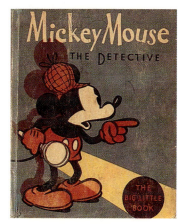
Mickey Mouse
The Detective
© 1934, book #1139.
$50

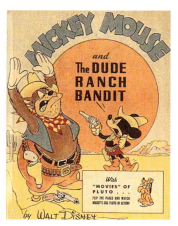
Mickey Mouse and the
Dude Ranch Bandit
© 1943, book #1471.
$40

BIG LITTLE BOOKS / BETTER LITTLE BOOKS
Whitman

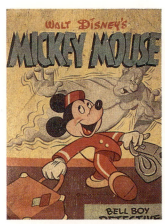

Mickey Mouse
Bell Boy Detective
© 1945, book #1483.
$40

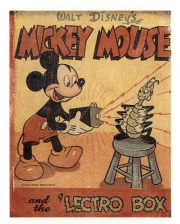

Mickey Mouse and the
'Lectro Box
© 1946, book #1413.
$45

Mickey Mouse and the
Magic Lamp
© 1942, book #1429.
$45

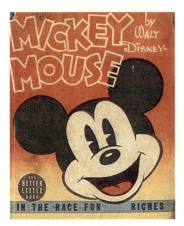

Mickey Mouse in the
Race for Riches
© 1938, book #1476.
$55

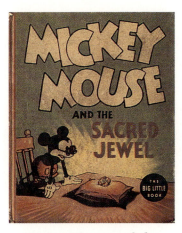

Mickey Mouse and the
Sacred Jewel
© 1936, book #1187.
$60

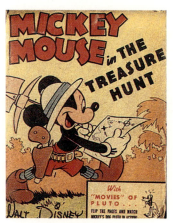

Mickey Mouse in the
Treasure Hunt
© 1941, book #1401.
$50

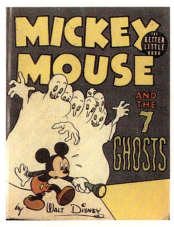

Mickey Mouse
and the 7 Ghosts
© 1940, book #1475.
$50

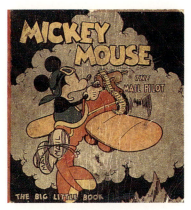

Mickey Mouse
The Mail Pilot, © 1933,
paperback, book #731.
$55

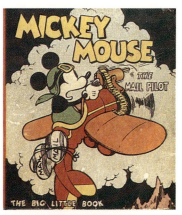

Mickey Mouse
The Mail Pilot
© 1933, book #731.
$65

BIG LITTLE BOOKS / BETTER LITTLE BOOKS
Whitman

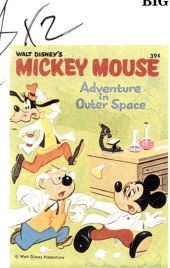

Mickey Mouse Adventure
in Outer Space
© 1968, book #5750.
$15

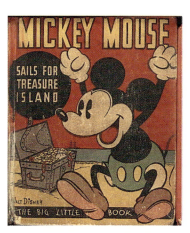

Mickey Mouse Sails for
Treasure Island
© 1933, book #750.
$65

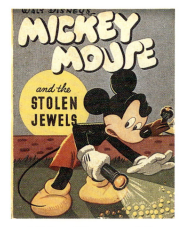

Mickey Mouse and the
Stolen Jewels
© 1949, book #1464.
$45

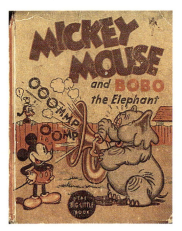

Mickey Mouse and Bobo
the Elephant
© 1935, book #1160.
$50

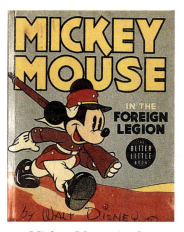

Mickey Mouse in the
Foreign Legion
© 1940, book #1428.
$45

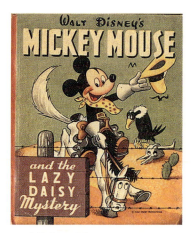

Mickey Mouse and the
Lazy Daisy Mystery
© 1947, book #1433.
$40

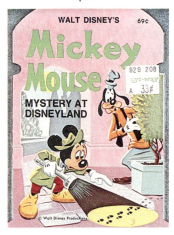

Mickey Mouse Mystery
at Disneyland
© 1975, book #5770.
$5

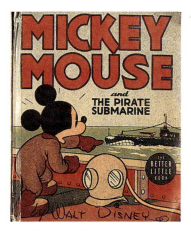

Mickey Mouse and the
Pirate Submarine
© 1939, book #1463.
$50

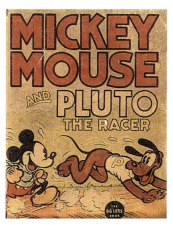

Mickey Mouse and
Pluto The Racer
© 1936, book #1128.
$55

BIG LITTLE BOOKS / BETTER LITTLE BOOKS
Whitman

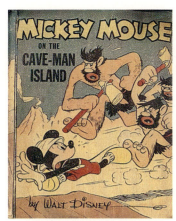

Mickey Mouse on the
Cave-Man Island
© 1944, book #1499.
$45

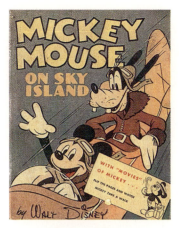

Mickey Mouse
on Sky Island
© 1941, book #1417.
$50

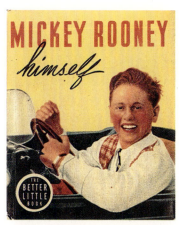

Mickey Rooney Himself
© 1939, book #1427.
$25

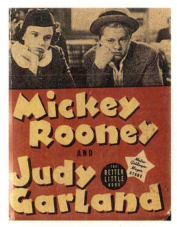

Mickey Rooney and
Judy Garland
© 1941, book #1493.
$25

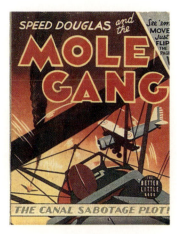

Mole Gang The Canal
Sabotage Plot!
© 1941, book #1455.
$20

Moon Mullins and Ka Yo
© 1933, book #746.
$35

Moon Mullins and Ka Yo
© 1933, giveaway.
$25

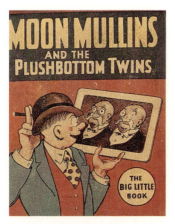

Moon Mullins and the
Plushbottom Twins
© 1935, book #1134.
$40

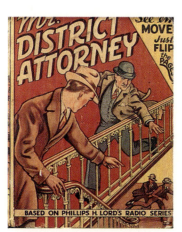

Mr. District Attorney
© 1941, book #1408.
$20

BIG LITTLE BOOKS / BETTER LITTLE BOOKS
Whitman

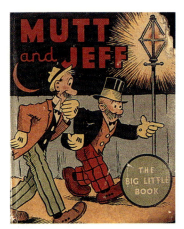

Mutt and Jeff
© 1936, book #1113.
$50

Myra North Special Nurse
and Foreign Spies
© 1938, book #1497.
$20

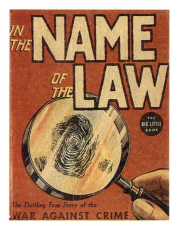

In The Name of the Law
© 1937, book #1155.
$30

Nancy Has Fun
© 1944, book #1487.
$25

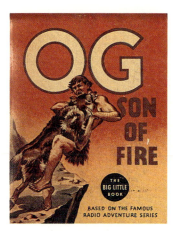

OG Son of Fire
© 1936, book #1115.
$30

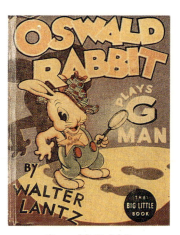

Oswald Rabbit
Plays G Man
© 1937, book #1403.
$30

Our Gang Adventures
© 1948, book #1456.
$20

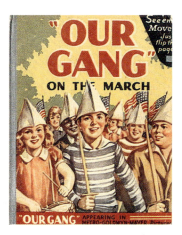

Our Gang on the March
© 1942, book #1451.
$25

Pat Nelson Ace
of Test Pilots
© 1937, book #1445.
$15

BIG LITTLE BOOKS / BETTER LITTLE BOOKS
Whitman

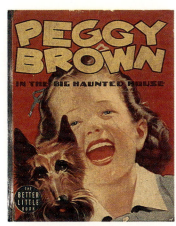

Peggy Brown in the
Big Haunted House
© 1940, book #1491.
$15

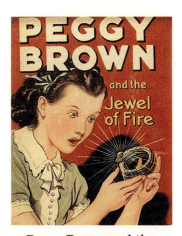

Peggy Brown and the
Jewel of Fire
© 1943, book #1463.
$15

Peggy Brown and the
Mystery Basket
© 1941, book #1411.
$40

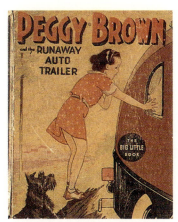

Peggy Brown and the
Runaway Auto Trailer
book #1427.
$15

Peggy Brown and the
Secret Treasure
© 1947, book #1423.
$15

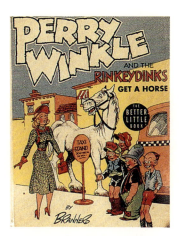

Perry Winkle and the
Rinkeydinks Get A Horse
© 1938, book #1497.
$25

The Phantom and
Desert Justice
© 1941, book #1421.
$40

The Phantom and the
Girl of Mystery
© 1947, book #1416.
$35

The Phantom and the
Sign of the Skull
© 1939, book #1474.
$45

BIG LITTLE BOOKS / BETTER LITTLE BOOKS
Whitman

The Return of
The Phantom
© 1942, book #1489.
$45

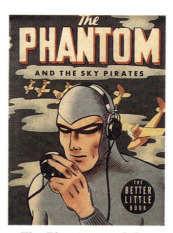

The Phantom and the
Sky Pirates
© 1945, book #1468.
$45

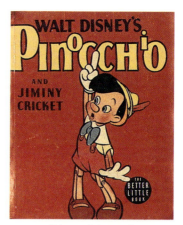

Pinocchio and
Jiminy Cricket,
The Walt Disney Co.
© 1940, book #1435.
$40

The Pink Panther
Adventures
© 1976, book #5776.
$5

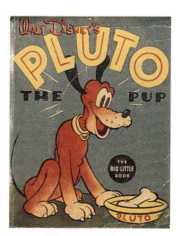

Pluto The Pup
© 1938, book #1467.
$25

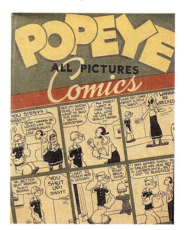

Popeye
book #1406.
$35

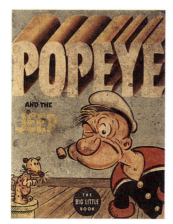

Popeye and the Jeep
© 1937, book #1405.
$40

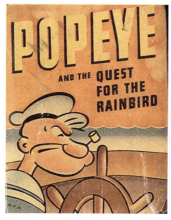

Popeye and the Quest
for the Rainbird
© 1943, book #1459.
$30

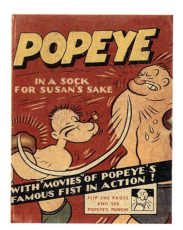

Popeye in a Sock for
Susan's Sake
© 1940, book #1485.
$35

BIG LITTLE BOOKS / BETTER LITTLE BOOKS
Whitman

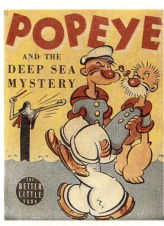

Popeye and the
Deep Sea Mystery
© 1939, book #1499.
$35

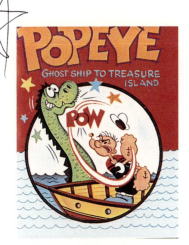

Popeye Ghost Ship To
Treasure Island
© 1967, book #5755.
$15

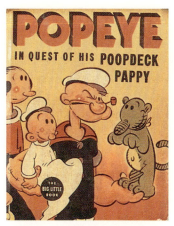

Popeye In Quest of His
Poopdeck Pappy
© 1937, book #1450.
$45

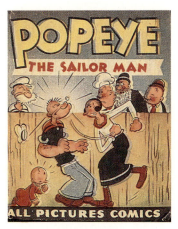

Popeye The Sailor Man
book #1422.
$30

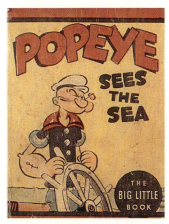

Popeye Sees The Sea
© 1936, book #1163.
$50

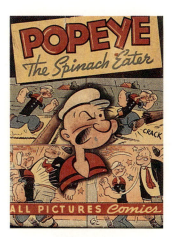

Popeye
The Spinach Eater
© 1945, book #1480.
$30

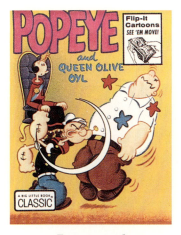

Popeye and
Queen Olive Oyl
© 1973, book #5761.
$5

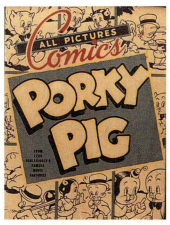

Porky Pig
© 1942, book #1408.
$35

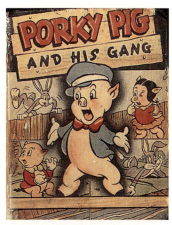

Porky Pig and His Gang
© 1946, book #1404.
$30

BIG LITTLE BOOKS / BETTER LITTLE BOOKS
Whitman

Powder Smoke Range
© 1935, book #1176.
$25

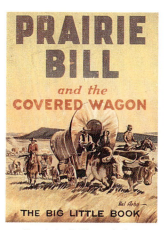

Prairie Bill and the
Covered Wagon
© 1934, book #758.
$20

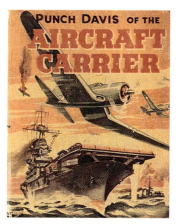

Punch Davis of the
Aircraft Carrier
© 1945, book #1440.
$15

Radio Patrol
© 1935, book #1142.
$20

Radio Patrol and
Big Dan's Mobsters
© 1940, book #1498.
$20

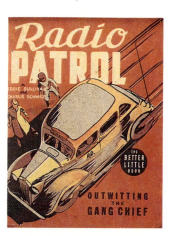

Radio Patrol Outwitting
the Gang Chief
© 1939, book #1496.
$20

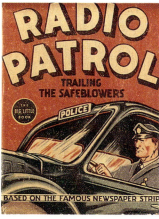

Radio Patrol Trailing
the Safeblowers
© 1937, book #1173.
$15

The Range Busters
© 1942, book #1441.
$20

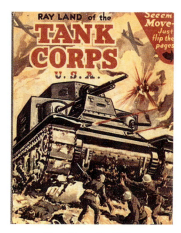

Ray Land of the
Tank Corps U.S.A.
© 1942, book #1447.
$25

BIG LITTLE BOOKS / BETTER LITTLE BOOKS
Whitman

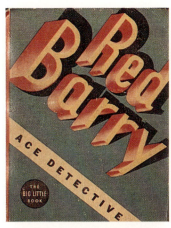

Red Barry Ace Detective
© 1935, book #1157.
$25

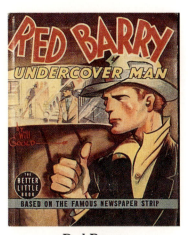

Red Barry
Undercover Man
© 1939, book #1426.
$25

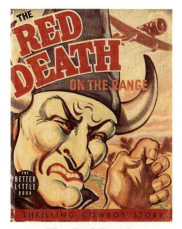

The Red Death
on the Range
© 1940, book #1449.
$30

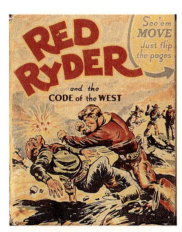

Red Ryder and the
Code of the West
© 1941, book #1427.
$30

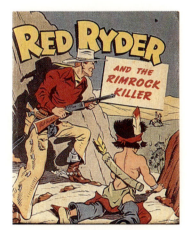

Red Ryder and the
Rimrock Killer
© 1945, book #1443.
$25

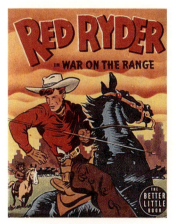

Red Ryder in
War on the Range
© 1945, book #1473.
$25

Red Ryder and
Circus Luck
© 1946, book #1466.
$25

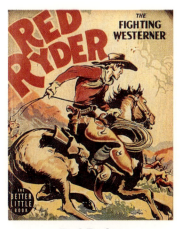

Red Ryder
The Fighting Westerner
© 1940, book #1440.
$30

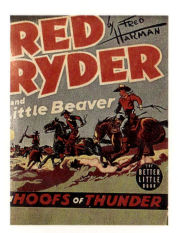

Red Ryder and
Little Beaver
© 1939, book #1400.
$35

BIG LITTLE BOOKS / BETTER LITTLE BOOKS
Whitman

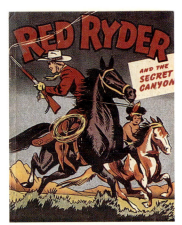

Red Ryder and
the Secret Canyon
© 1947, book #1454.
$25

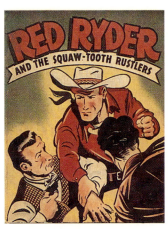

Red Ryder and the
Squaw-Tooth Rustlers
© 1946, book #1414.
$25

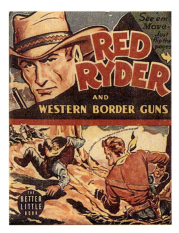

Red Ryder and
Western Border Guns
© 1942, book #1450.
$30

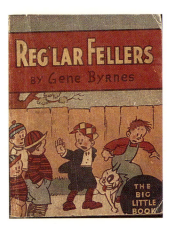

Reg'lar Fellers
© 1933, giveaway.
$25

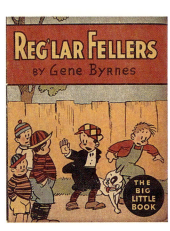

Reg'lar Fellers
© 1933, book #754.
$20

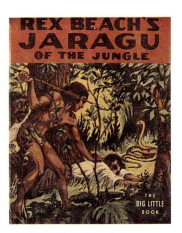

Rex Beach's Jaragu
of the Jungle
© 1937, book #1424.
$15

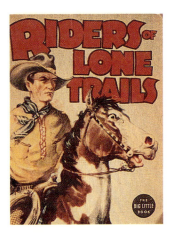

Riders of Lone Trails
© 1937, giveaway.
$15

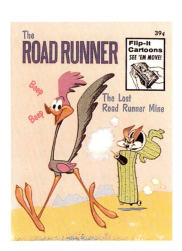

The Road Runner The
Lost Road Runner Mine
© 1974, book #5767.
$5

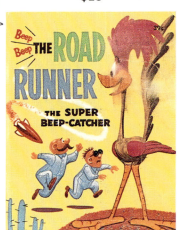

The Road Runner The
Super Beep-Catcher
© 1968, book #2023.
$5

BIG LITTLE BOOKS / BETTER LITTLE BOOKS
Whitman

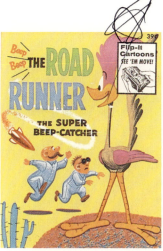

The Road Runner The
Super Beep-Catcher
© 1973, book #5759.
$5

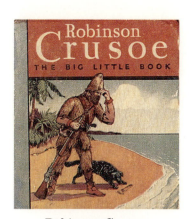

Robinson Crusoe
© 1933, book #719.
$30

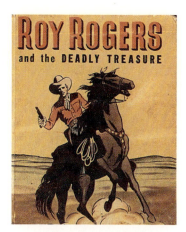

Roy Rogers and the
Deadly Treasure
© 1947, book #1437.
$25

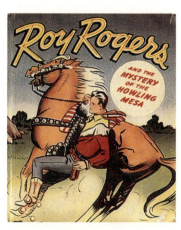

Roy Rogers and the
Mystery of the
Howling Mesa
© 1948, book #1448.
$25

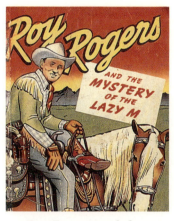

Roy Rogers and the
Mystery of the Lazy M
© 1949, book #1462.
$25

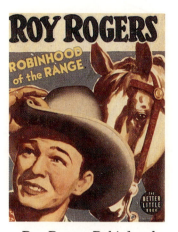

Roy Rogers Robinhood
of the Range
© 1942, book #1460.
$30

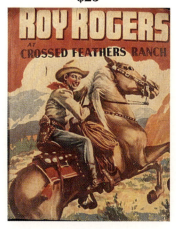

Roy Rogers at Crossed
Feathers Ranch
© 1945, book #1494.
$20

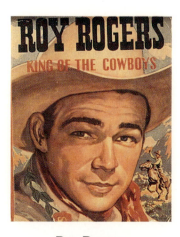

Roy Rogers
King of the Cowboys
© 1943, book #1476.
$25

Secret Agent X-9
© 1936, book #1144.
$25

BIG LITTLE BOOKS / BETTER LITTLE BOOKS
Whitman

Secret Agent X-9 and
the Mad Assassin
© 1938, book #1472.
$25

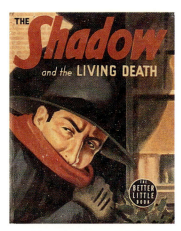

The Shadow and the
Living Death
© 1940, book #1430.
$55

The Shadow and The
Master of Evil
© 1941, book #1443.
$55

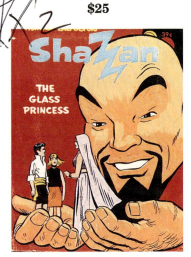

Shazzan The
Glass Princess
© 1968, book #2024.
$10

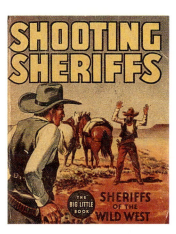

Shooting Sheriffs
Sheriffs of the Wild West
© 1936, book #1195.
$15

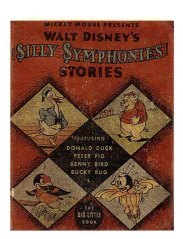

Silly Symphonies Stories
© 1936, book #1111.
$60

Skeezix on His Own
in the Big City
© 1941, book #1419.
$30

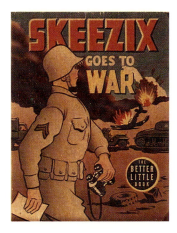

Skeezix Goes To War
© 1938, book #1408.
$30

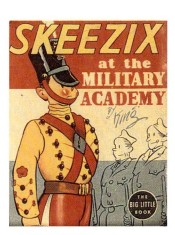

Skeezix at the
Military Academy
© 1944, book #1414.
$25

BIG LITTLE BOOKS / BETTER LITTLE BOOKS
Whitman

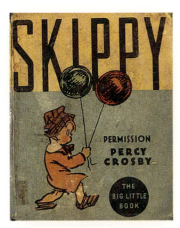

Skippy
© 1934, book #761.
$25

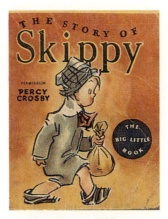

The Story of Skippy
© 1934, a giveaway.
$35

Skyroads w/Clipper Williams
of the Flying Legion
© 1938, book #1439.
$25

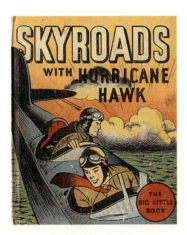

Skyroads with
Hurricane Hawk
© 1936, book #1127.
$35

Smilin' Jack
© 1945, book #1464.
$25

Smilin' Jack and the
Stratosphere Ascent
© 1937, book #1152.
$35

Smilin' Jack and the
Escape from Death Rock
© 1943, book #1445.
$25

Smilin' Jack Flying
High with Downwind
© 1942, book #1412.
$30

Smilin' Jack Speed Pilot
© 1941, book #1473.
$30

BIG LITTLE BOOKS / BETTER LITTLE BOOKS
Whitman

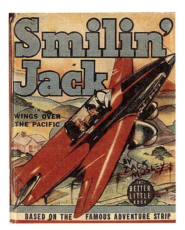

Smilin' Jack Wings Over
The Pacific
© 1939, book #1416.
$25

Smitty in Going Native
© 1938, book #1477.
$15

Smitty Golden Gloves
Tournament
© 1934, a giveaway.
$30

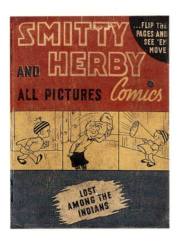

Smitty and Herby
© 1941, book #1404.
$20

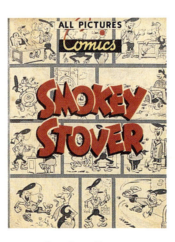

Smokey Stover
© 1942, book #1413.
$30

Smokey Stover
The Foo Fighter
© 1938, book #1421.
$30

Smokey Stover The
Foolish Foo Fighter
© 1945, book #1481.
$25

Snow White and the
Seven Dwarfs
© 1938, book #1460.
$40

Sombrero Pete
© 1936, book #1136.
$20

BIG LITTLE BOOKS / BETTER LITTLE BOOKS
Whitman

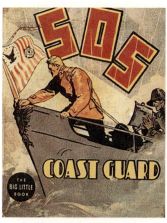

SOS Coast Guard
© 1936, book #1191.
$25

Space Ghost The
Sorceress of Cyba-3
© 1968, book #2016.
$10

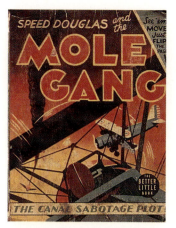

Speed Douglas and the
Mole Gang The Canal
Sabotage Plot
© 1941, book #1455.
$20

Spider-Man
Zaps Mr. Zodiac
© 1976, book #5779.
$5

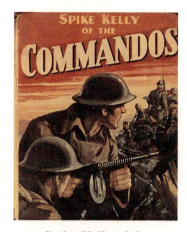

Spike Kelly of the
Commandos
© 1943, book #1467.
$15

The Spy
© 1936, book #768.
$30

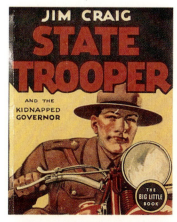

Jim Craig State Trooper
and the Kidnapped Governor
© 1938, book #1466.
$25

Steve Hunter of the
U.S. Coast Guard
Under Secret Orders
© 1942, book #1426.
$30

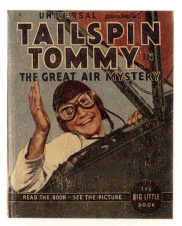

Tailspin Tommy The
Great Air Mystery
© 1936, book #1184.
$30

BIG LITTLE BOOKS / BETTER LITTLE BOOKS
Whitman

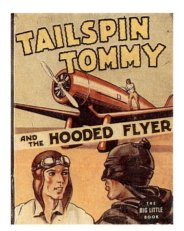

Tailspin Tommy and the
Hooded Flyer
© 1937, book #1423.
$25

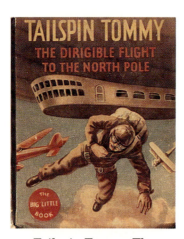

Tailspin Tommy The
Dirigible Flight to the
North Pole
© 1934, book #1124.
$30

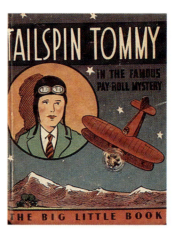

Tailspin Tommy in the
Famous Pay-Roll Mystery
© 1933, book #747.
$35

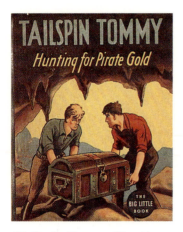

Tailspin Tommy Hunting
for Pirate Gold
© 1935, book #1172.
$30

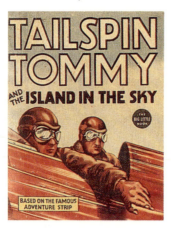

Tailspin Tommy and the
Island in the Sky
© 1936, book #1110.
$25

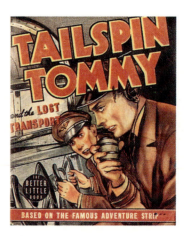

Tailspin Tommy and the
Lost Transport
© 1939, book #1413.
$20

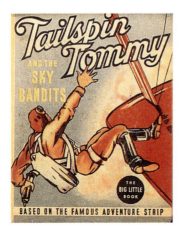

Tailspin Tommy and the
Sky Bandits
© 1938, book #1494.
$25

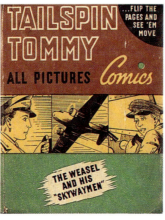

Tailspin Tommy The
Weasel and His Skywaymen
book #1410.
$20

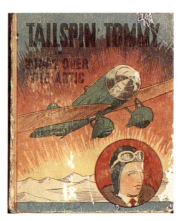

Tailspin Tommy in
Wings Over the Artic
© 1935, a giveaway.
$40

BIG LITTLE BOOKS / BETTER LITTLE BOOKS
Whitman

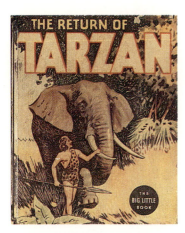

The Return of Tarzan
© 1936, book #1102.
$40

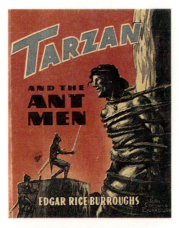

Tarzan and the Ant Men
© 1945, book #1444.
$35

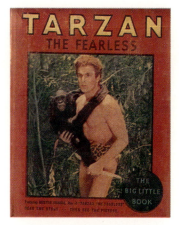

Tarzan The Fearless
© 1934, book #769.
$40

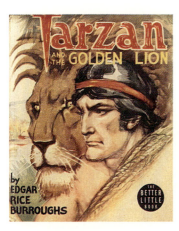

Tarzan and the
Golden Lion
© 1943, book #1448.
$35

Tarzan Lord
of the Jungle
© 1946, book #1407.
$30

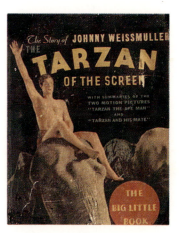

Tarzan of the Screen
© 1934, book #778.
$40

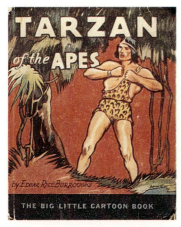

Tarzan of the Apes
© 1933, book #744,
(1st book of Tarzan).
$70

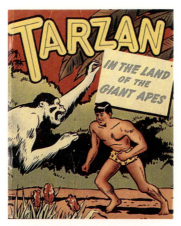

Tarzan in the Land of
the Giant Apes
© 1949, book #1467.
$25

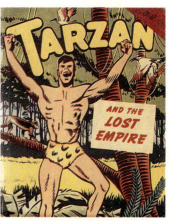

Tarzan and the
Lost Empire
© 1948, book #1442.
$25

49

BIG LITTLE BOOKS / BETTER LITTLE BOOKS
Whitman

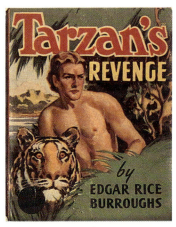

Tarzan's Revenge
© 1938, book #1488.
$35

Tarzan The Terrible
© 1942, book #1453.
$35

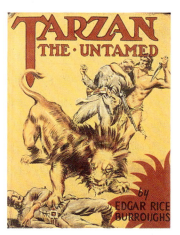

Tarzan The Untamed
© 1941, book #1452.
$30

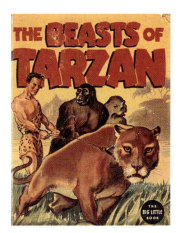

The Beasts of Tarzan
© 1937, book #1410.
$40

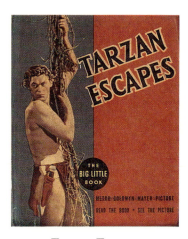

Tarzan Escapes
© 1936, book #1182.
$40

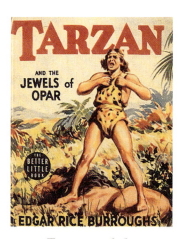

Tarzan and the
Jewels of Opar
© 1940, book #1495.
$35

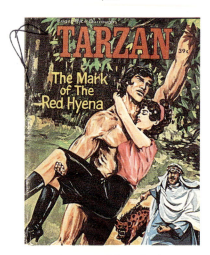

Tarzan The Mark
of the Red Hyena
© 1967, book #2005.
$10

The Tarzan Twins
© 1934, book #770.
$100

Terry and War
in the Jungle
© 1946, book #1420.
$20

BIG LITTLE BOOKS / BETTER LITTLE BOOKS
Whitman

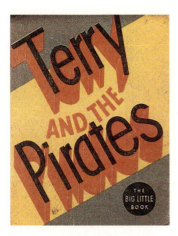
Terry and the Pirates
© 1935, book #1156.
$35

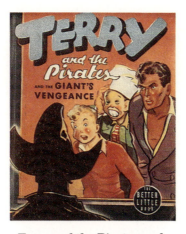
Terry and the Pirates and the Giant's Vengeance
© 1939, book #1446.
$25

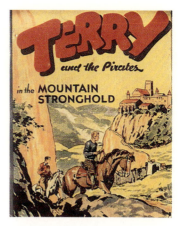
Terry and the Pirates in the Mountain Stronghold
© 1941, book #1499.
$25

Terry and the Pirates The Plantation Mystery
© 1942, book #1436.
$25

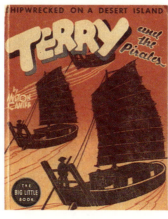
Terry and the Pirates Shipwrecked on a Desert Island © 1938, book #1412.
$30

Terry Lee Flight Officer U.S.A.
© 1944, book #1492.
$20

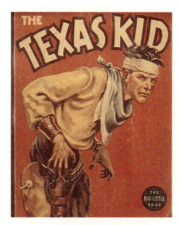
The Texas Kid
© 1937, book #1429.
$15

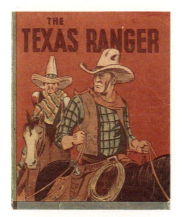
The Texas Ranger
© 1936, a giveaway.
$20

The Texas Ranger
© 1936, book #1135.
$15

BIG LITTLE BOOKS / BETTER LITTLE BOOKS
Whitman

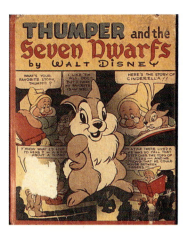

Thumper and the
Seven Dwarfs
© 1944, book #1409.
$30

Tillie the Toiler and the
Wild Man of
Desert Island
© 1941, book #1442.
$20

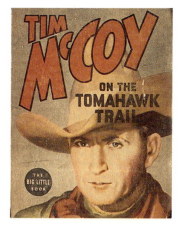

Tim McCoy on the
Tomahawk Trail
© 1937, book #1436.
$30

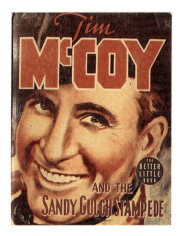

Tim McCoy and the
Sandy Gulch Stampede
© 1939, book #1490.
$30

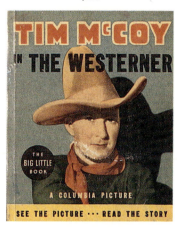

Tim McCoy in
The Westerner
© 1936, book #1193.
$30

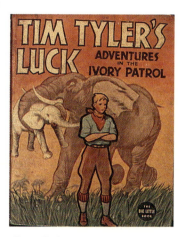

Tim Tyler's Luck Adventures in the Ivory Patrol
© 1937, book #1140.
$15

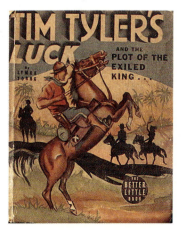

Tim Tyler's Luck and the
Plot of the Exiled King
© 1939, book #1479.
$20

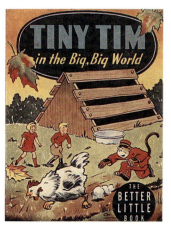

Tiny Tim in the
Big, Big World
© 1945, book #1472.
$20

Tiny Tim and the
Mechanical Men
© 1937, book #1172.
$25

BIG LITTLE BOOKS / BETTER LITTLE BOOKS
Whitman

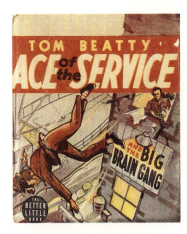

Tom Beatty Ace of the
Service and the
Big Brain Gang
© 1939, book #1420.
$20

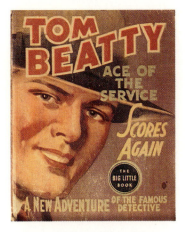

Tom Beatty Ace of the
Service Scores Again
© 1937, book #1165.
$25

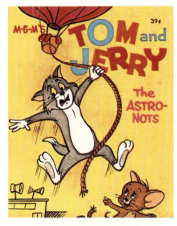

Tom and Jerry The
Astro-nots
© 1969, book #2030.
$5

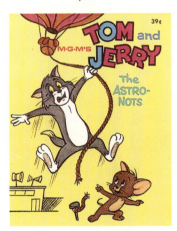

Tom and Jerry The
Astro-nots
© 1969, book #5769.
$5

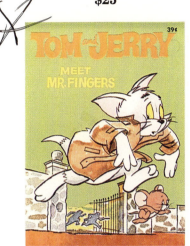

Tom and Jerry Meet
Mr. Fingers
© 1967, book #2006.
$5

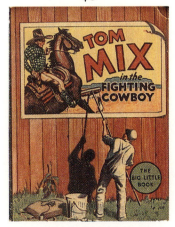

Tom and Jerry Meet
Mr. Fingers
© 1967, book #5752.
$5

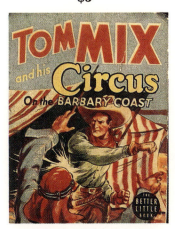

Tom Mix and his Circus
on the Barbary Coast
© 1940, book #1482.
$30

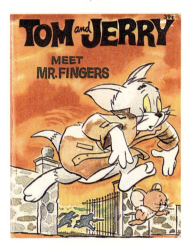

Tom Mix in the
Fighting Cowboy
© 1935, book #1144.
$35

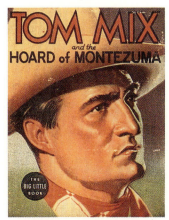

Tom Mix and the
Hoard of Montezuma
© 1937, book #1462.
$35

BIG LITTLE BOOKS / BETTER LITTLE BOOKS
Whitman

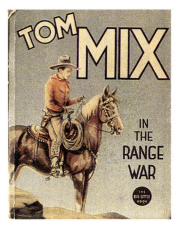

**Tom Mix in the
Range War**
© 1937, book #1166.
$35

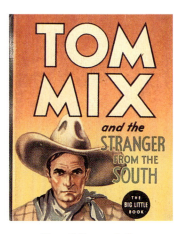

**Tom Mix and the
Stranger from the South**
© 1936, book #1183.
$35

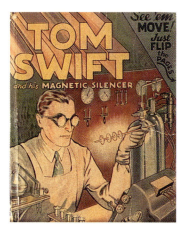

**Tom Swift and his
Magnetic Silencer**
© 1941, book #1437.
$25

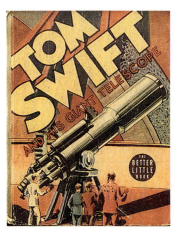

**Tom Swift and His
Giant Telescope**
© 1939, book #1485.
$30

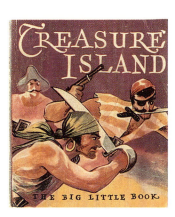

Treasure Island
© 1933, book #720.
$25

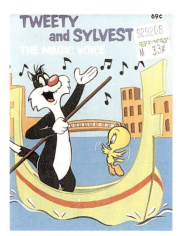

**Tweety and Sylvester
The Magic Voice**
© 1976, book #5777.
$5

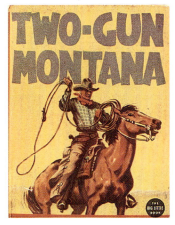

Two-Gun Montana
© 1936, book #1104.
$15

**Uncle Don's
Strange Adventures**
© 1936, book #1114.
$25

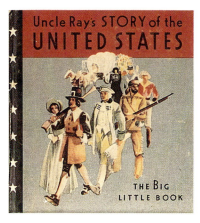

**Uncle Ray's Story of the
United States**
© 1934, book #722.
$25

BIG LITTLE BOOKS / BETTER LITTLE BOOKS
Whitman

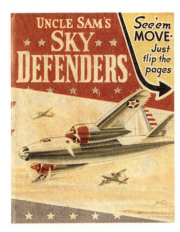

Uncle Sam's
Sky Defenders
© 1941, book #1461.
$20

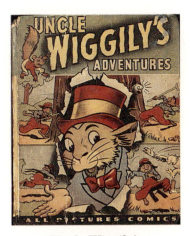

Uncle Wiggily's
Adventures
© 1946, book #1405.
$20

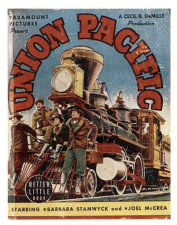

Union Pacific
© 1939, book #1411.
$25

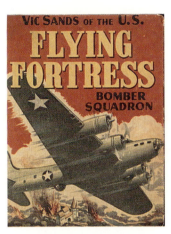

Vic Sands of the U.S.
Flying Fortress
© 1944, book #1455.
$20

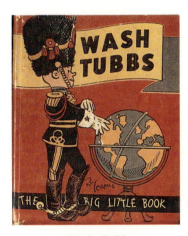

Wash Tubbs
© 1934, book #751.
$30

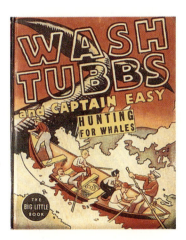

Wash Tubbs and Captain
Easy Hunting for Whales
© 1938, book #1455.
$25

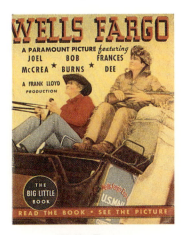

Wells Fargo
© 1938, book #1471.
$20

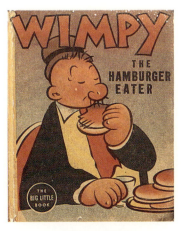

Wimpy The
Hamburger Eater
© 1938, book #1458.
$35

Wings of the U.S.A.
© 1940, book #1407.
$20

BIG LITTLE BOOKS / BETTER LITTLE BOOKS
Whitman

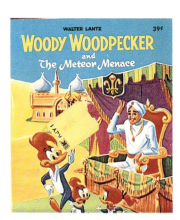

Woody Woodpecker and
The Meteor Menace
© 1961, book #5753.
$5

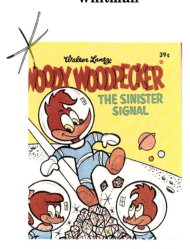

Woody Woodpecker The
Sinister Signal
© 1969, book #2028.
$5

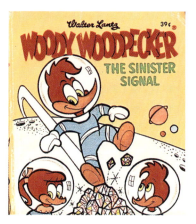

Woody Woodpecker The
Sinister Signal
© 1969, book #5763.
$5

Zane Grey's King of the
Royal Mounted
© 1935, a giveaway.
$25

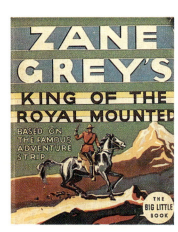

Zane Grey's King of the
Royal Mounted
© 1936, book #1103.
$30

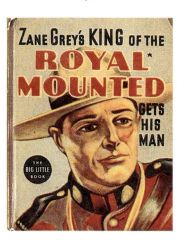

Zane Grey's King of the Royal
Mounted Gets His Man
© 1936, book #1452.
$30

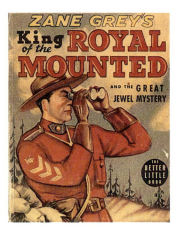

Zane Grey's King of the
Royal Mounted and the
Great Jewel Mystery
© 1937, book #1486.
$30

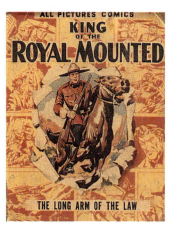

King of the Royal Mounted
The Long Arm of the Law
© 1943, book #1405.
$25

Zane Grey's Tex Thorne
Comes Out of the West
© 1937, book #1440.
$20

THE BIG LITTLE BOOK

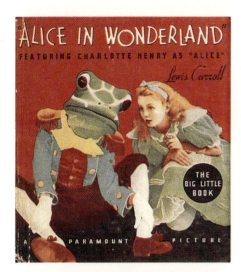

Alice In Wonderland
© 1934, book #759, 4⁵⁄₈" x 5¹⁄₈".
$30

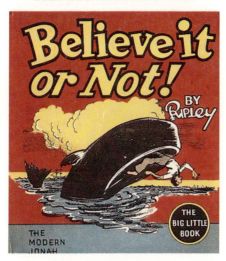

Believe It Or Not!
© 1931, book #760, 4⁵⁄₈" x 5¹⁄₈".
$35

Betty Boop in Snow White
© 1934, book #1119, 4⁵⁄₈" x 5¹⁄₈".
$35

Buck Jones in the Fighting Code
© 1934, book #1104, 4⁵⁄₈" x 5¹⁄₈".
$25

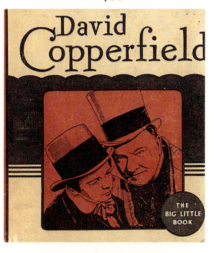

David Copperfield
© 1934, paperback, 4⁵⁄₁₆" x 5".
$30

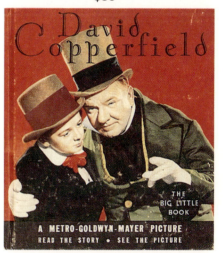

David Copperfield
© 1934, book #1148, 4⁵⁄₈" x 5¹⁄₈".
$35

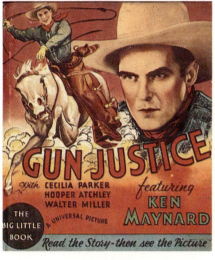

Gun Justice
© 1934, book #776, 4⁵⁄₈" x 5¹⁄₈".
$30

Gun Justice
© 1934, book #776,
paperback, 4⁵⁄₁₆" x 5".
$25

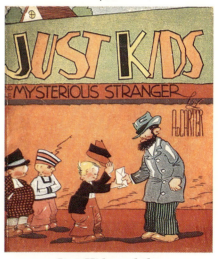

Just Kids and the
Mysterious Stranger
© 1934, book #1094, 4⁵⁄₈" x 5¹⁄₈".
$25

THE BIG LITTLE BOOK

Lions and Tigers with the
Sensational Dare-Devil Clyde Beatty
© 1934, book #653, 4⅝" x 5⅛".
$20

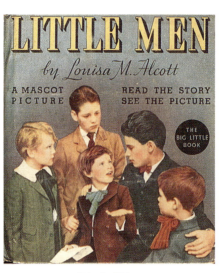

Little Men
© 1934, book #1160, 4⅝" x 5⅛".
$30

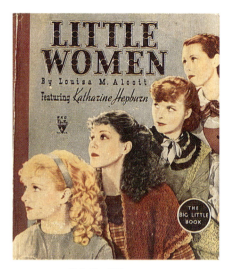

Little Women
© 1934, book #757, 4⅝" x 5⅛".
$35

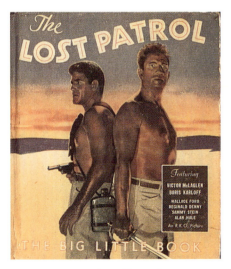

The Lost Patrol
© 1934, book #753, 4⅝" x 5⅛".
$25

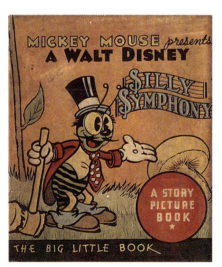

Mickey Mouse Presents A
Walt Disney Silly Symphony
© 1934, book #756, 4⅝" x 5⅛".
$35

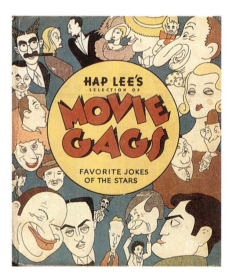

Movie Gags
© 1935, book #1145, 4⅝" x 5⅛".
$30

THE BIG LITTLE BOOK

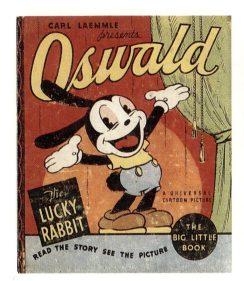

Oswald The Lucky Rabbit
© 1934, book #1109, 4⅝" x 5⅛".
$20

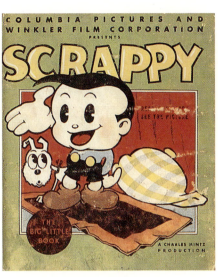

Scrappy
© 1934, book #1122, 4⅝" x 5⅛".
$25

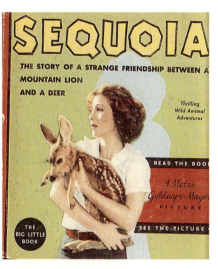

Sequoia The Story of a Strange
Friendship Between
A Mountain Lion and a Deer
© 1935, book #1161, 4⅝" x 5⅛".
$25

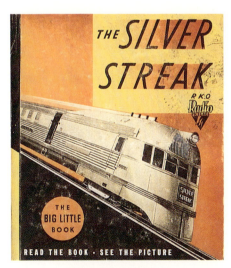

The Silver Streak
© 1935, book #1155, 4⅝" x 5⅛".
$20

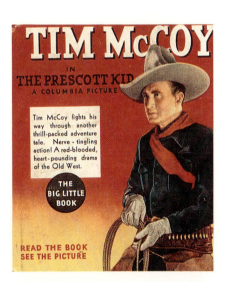

Tim McCoy in The Prescott Kid
© 1935, book #1152, 4⅝" x 5⅛".
$25

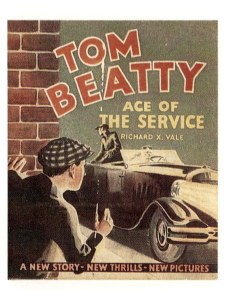

Tom Beatty Ace of The Service
© 1934, book #723, 4⅝" x 5⅛".
$30

THE BIG LITTLE BOOK

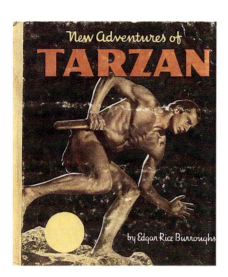

Tarzan, The New Adventures of
© 1935, book #1180,
paperback, 4⁵⁄₁₆" x 5".
$35

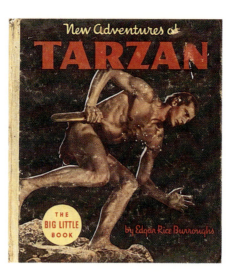

Tarzan, The New Adventures of
© 1935, book #1180, 4⅝" x 5⅛".
$35

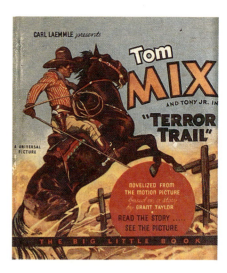

Tom Mix and Tony Jr.
in Terror Trail
© 1934, book #762, 4⅝" x 5⅛".
$30

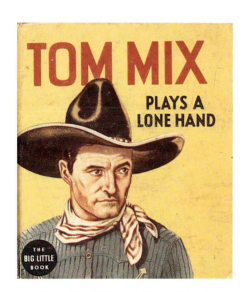

Tom Mix Plays A Lone Hand
© 1935, book #1173, 4⅝" x 5⅛".
$40

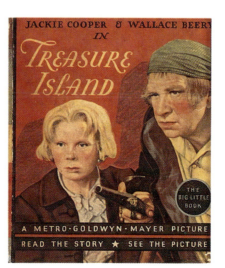

Treasure Island, Jackie Cooper &
Wallace Berry in
© 1934, book #1141, 4⅝" x 5⅛".
$40

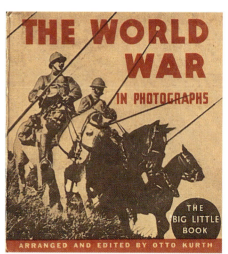

The World War in Photographs
© 1934, book #779L, 4⅝" x 5⅛".
$35

THE BIG LITTLE BOOK TV SERIES

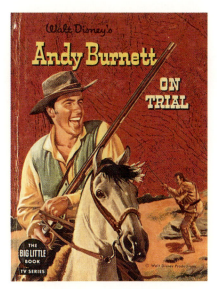
Andy Burnett On Trial
© 1958, book #1645.

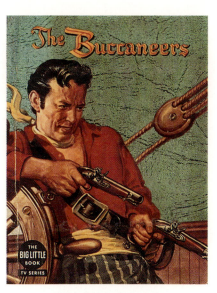
The Buccaneers
© 1958, book #1646.

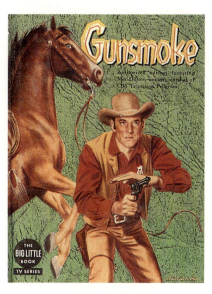
Gunsmoke
© 1958, book #1647.

The Adventures of Jim Bowie
© 1958, book #1648.

Sir Lancelot
© 1958, book #1649.

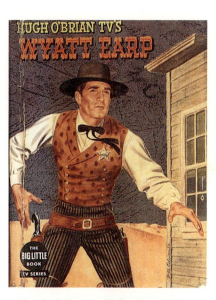
Hugh O'Brian TV's Wyatt Earp
© 1958, book #1644.

These books came in a set of six.

$180 for the set

NEW LITTLE BETTER BOOKS

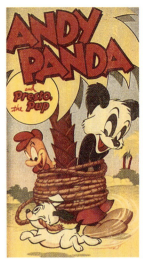
Andy Panda and Presto the Pup, © 1949, 3⅛" x 5¼".
$20

Blondie and Dagwood Some Fun, © 1949, 3⅛" x 5¼".
$20

Bugs Bunny and the Giant Brothers, © 1949, 3⅛" x 5¼".
$30

Cinderella and the Magic Wand, © 1950, 3⅛" x 5¼".
$50

Brer Rabbit Tales By Uncle Remus, © 1949, 3⅛" x 5¼".
$35

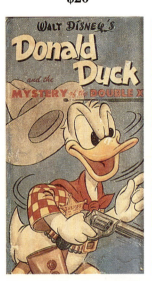
Donald Duck and the Mystery of the Double X, © 1949, 3⅛" x 5¼".
$45

Gene Autry and the Bandits of Silver Tip, © 1949, 3⅛" x 5¼".
$25

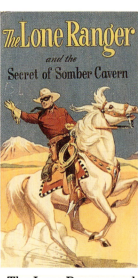
The Lone Ranger and the Secret of Somber Cavern, © 1950, 3⅛" x 5¼".
$35

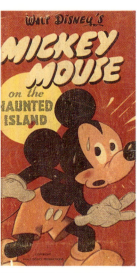
Mickey Mouse on the Haunted Island, © 1950, 3⅛" x 5¼".
$30

Red Ryder Acting Sheriff, © 1949, 3⅛" x 5¼".
$25

Roy Rogers and the Snowbound Outlaws, © 1949, 3⅛" x 5¼".
$25

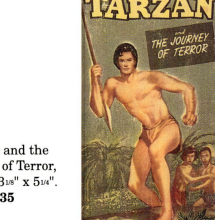
Tarzan and the Journey of Terror, © 1950, 3⅛" x 5¼".
$35

Whitman

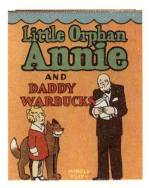
Little Orphan Annie
and Daddy Warbucks
© 1934, 2⅝" x 3⅝".

Little Orphan Annie
Finds Mickey
© 1934, 2⅝" x 3⅝".

Little Orphan Annie
at Happy Home
© 1934, 2⅝" x 3⅝".

This is the box
that the set of 6
Little Orphan Annie
books by Whitman came in.
$130 for the set w/box

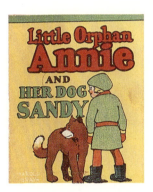
Little Orphan Annie
and Her Dog Sandy
© 1934, 2⅝" x 3⅝".

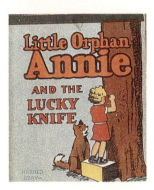
Little Orphan Annie
and the Lucky Knife
© 1934, 2⅝" x 3⅝".

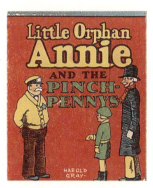
Little Orphan Annie
and the Pinch-
Pennys
© 1934, 2⅝" x 3⅝".

Junior G-Men
© 1939, 2½" x 3⅝".
$20

The Fighting Cowboy
of Nugget Gulch
© 1939, 2½" x 3⅝".
$15

Whitman

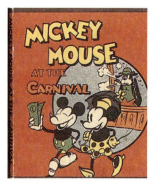
Mickey Mouse
at the Carnival
© 1934, 3⅛" x 3⅝".
$35

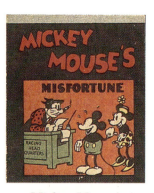
Mickey Mouse's
Misfortune
© 1934, 3⅛" x 3⅝".
$35

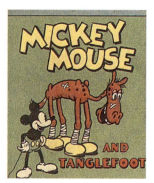
Mickey Mouse
and Tanglefoot
© 1934, 3⅛" x 3⅝".
$40

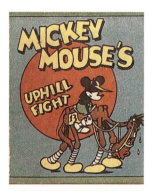
Mickey Mouse's
Uphill Fight
© 1934, 3⅛" x 3⅝".
$35

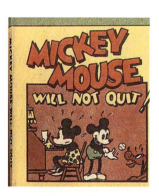
Mickey Mouse
Will Not Quit!
© 1934, 3⅛" x 3⅝".
$40

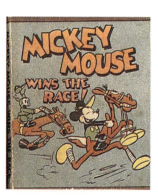
Mickey Mouse
Wins the Race!
© 1934, 3⅛" x 3⅝".
$40

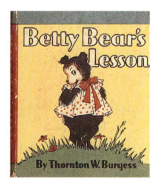
Betty Bear's Lesson
© 1930, 3⅛" x 3⅝".
$5

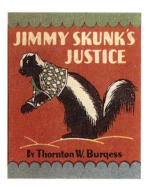
Jimmy Skunk's
Justice
© 1933, 3⅛" x 3⅝".
$5

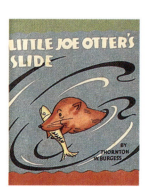
Little Joe Otter's Slide
© 1929, 3⅛" x 3⅝".
$5

Whitman

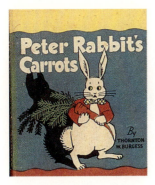

Peter Rabbit's Carrots
© 1933, 3 1/8" x 3 5/8".
$5

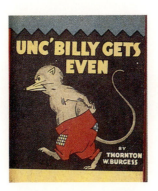

Unc' Billy Gets Even
© 1930, 3 1/8" x 3 5/8".
$5

Whitefoot's Secret
© 1930, 3 1/8" x 3 5/8".
$5

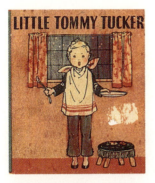

Little Tommy Tucker
© 1934, 3 1/8" x 3 1/2".
$20

Old King Cole
© 1934, 3 1/8" x 3 1/2".
$20

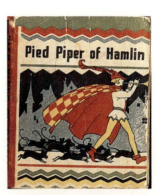

Pied Piper of Hamlin
© 1934, 3 1/8" x 3 1/2".
$20

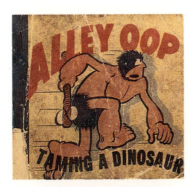

Alley Oop Taming
A Dinosaur © 1938,
3 1/2" x 3 5/8". This book
had an Advertisement
for Pan-Am Motor Oils
on the back of cover.
$35

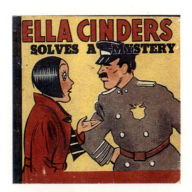

Ella Cinders
Solves A Mystery
© 1938, 3 1/2" x 3 5/8".
This book had an
Advertisement for
Pan-Am Motor Oils on
the back of cover.
$25

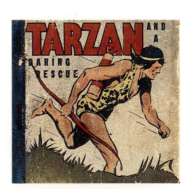

Tarzan and a Daring
Rescue, © 1938,
3 1/2" x 3 5/8". This book
had an Advertisement
for Pan-Am Motor Oils
on the back of cover.
$45

Whitman

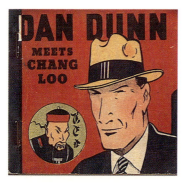

Dan Dunn Meets
Chang Loo © 1938,
3½" x 3⅝". This book
had an Advertisement
for Pan-Am Motor Oils
on the back of cover.
$35

The Captain and the
Kids with Uncle Seltzer
© 1938, 3½" x 3⅝".
This book had an
Advertisement for
Pan-Am Motor Oils on
the back of cover.
$40

Dan Dunn Secret
Operative 48 on Case
No. 33, © 1938,
3½" x 3⅝". This book
had an Advertisement
for Pan-Am Motor Oils
on the back of cover.
$35

The Captain and the Kids
Boys Vill Be Boys © 1938,
3½" x 3⅝". This book had
an Advertisement for
Pan-Am Motor Oils on the
back of cover.
$35

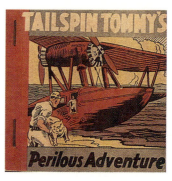

Tailspin Tommy's Perilous
Adventure, © 1934,
3½" x 3⅝". This book had
an Advertisement for Pan-
Am Motor Oils on the back
of cover.
$30

Chester Gump Finds The Hidden Treasure
© 1934, 3½" x 5⅝".
$40

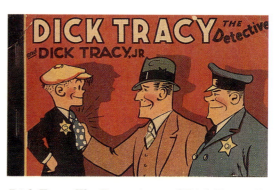

Dick Tracy The Detective and Dick Tracy, Jr.
© 1933, 3½" x 5⅝".
$60

TINY TALES

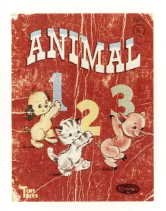
Animal 1 2 3,
© 1959, book #2952,
3 1/8" x 4 1/8".
$10

Animal Parade,
© 1959, book #2952,
3 1/8" x 4 1/8".
$10

Cowboy Bill,
© 1950, book #2952,
3 1/8" x 4 1/8".
$10

Five Fat Piggies,
© 1950, book #2952,
3 1/8" x 4 1/8".
$10

Hide and Seek,
© 1950, book #2952,
3 1/8" x 4 1/8".
$10

Telling Time,
© 1959, book #2952,
3 1/8" x 4 1/8".
$10

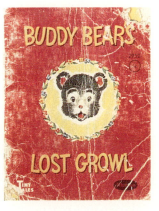
Buddy Bears
Lost Growl, © 1959,
book #2952, 3 1/8" x 4 1/8".
$10

Plush,
© 1956, book #2952,
3 1/8" x 4 1/8".
$10

Rover,
© 1954, book #2952,
3 1/8" x 4 1/8".
$10

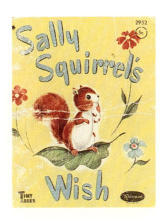
Sally Squirrel's Wish,
© 1950, book #2952,
3 1/8" x 4 1/8".
$10

Steve The Steam
Shovel, © 1950,
book #2952, 3 1/8" x 4 1/8".
$10

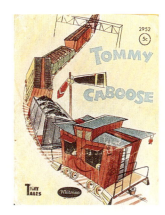
Tommy Caboose,
© 1950, book #2952,
3 1/8" x 4 1/8".
$10

A TOP-LINE COMIC

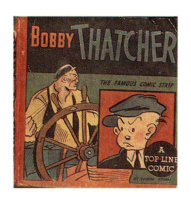

Bobby Thatcher
© 1935, 3⅝" x 3⅝".
$35

Broncho Bill, © 1935,
3⅝" x 4".
$25

Broncho Bill,
© 1935, 3⅝" x 3⅝".
$30

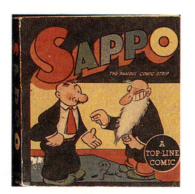

Sappo
© 1935, 3⅝" x 3⅝".
$35

RADIO PLAY SCRIPT

Dick Tracy and the
Invisible Man
© 1939, 3½" x 3⅝".
$50

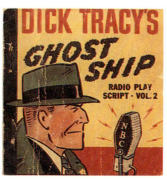

Dick Tracy's Ghost Ship,
© 1935, 3½" x 3⅝"..
$50

MISCELLANEOUS BOOKS

576 Pages of Mother Goose
book #725, 4⅛" x 5½". (Pages were
missing in front, no date was found).
$15

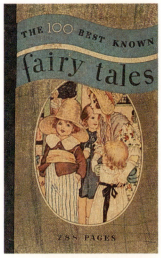

The 100 Best Known
Fairy Tales, 288 pages,
© 1933, book #712,
3½" x 5⁵⁄₁₆".
$15

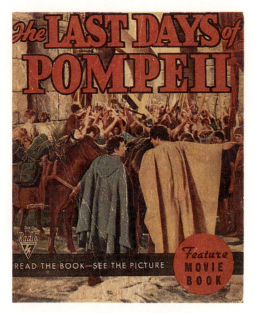

The Last Days of Pompeii
© 1935, book #1132, 5⅛" x 6⅛",
"A Feature Book".
$50

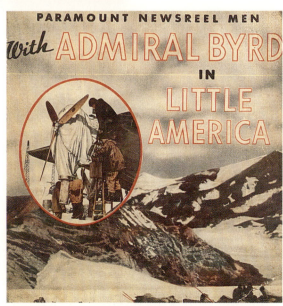

Paramount Newsreal Men with Admiral
Byrd in Little America
© 1934, 6 x 6⅛".
$20

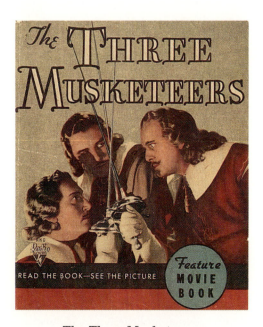

The Three Musketeers
© 1935, book #1131, 5⅛" x 6⅛",
"Feature Movie Book".
$50

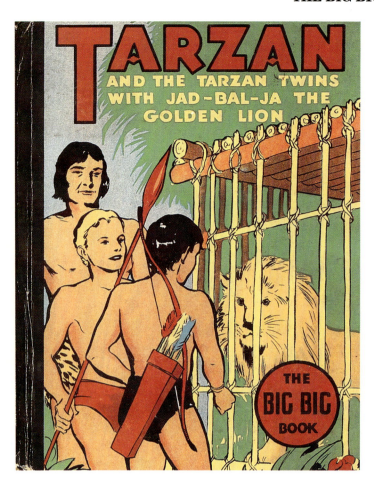

Tarzan and the Tarzan Twins with
Jad-Bal-Ja The Golden Lion,
© 1936, book #4056, 7½" x 9½".
$125

Buck Jones and the Night Riders
© 1937, book #4069, 7½" x 9½".
$100

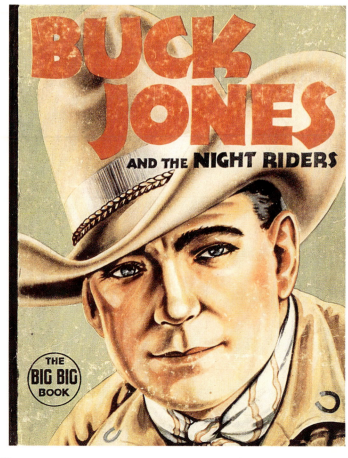

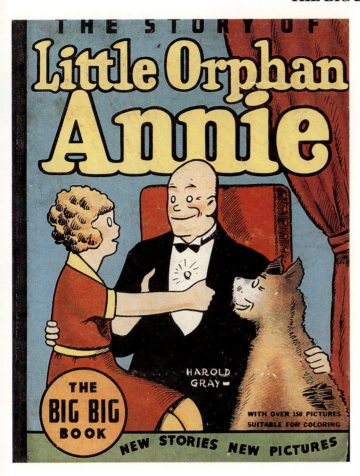

The Story of Little Orphan Annie
© 1934, book #4054, 7½" x 9½".
$110

Tom Mix and the Scourge of Paradise Valley
© 1937, book #4068, 7½" x 9½".
$70

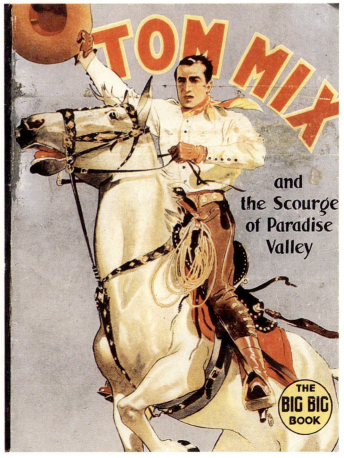

A FAST-ACTION STORY
Dell

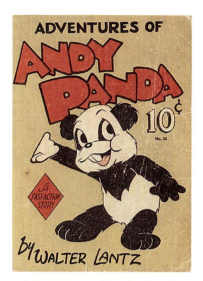

Adventures of Andy Panda
© 1942, 4" x 5½".
$30

Dan Dunn Secret Operative
48 and the Zeppelin of Doom
© 1938, 4" x 5½".
$25

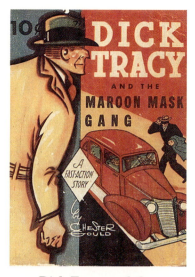

Dick Tracy and the
Maroon Mask Gang
© 1938, 4" x 5½".
$50

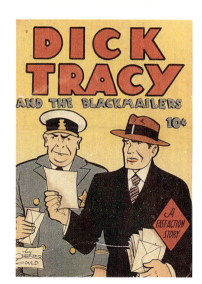

Dick Tracy and
The Blackmailers
© 1939, 4" x 5½".
$45

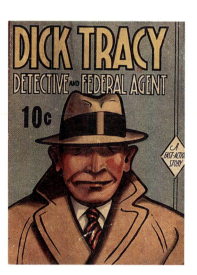

Dick Tracy Detective and
Federal Agent
© 1936, 4" x 5½".
$45

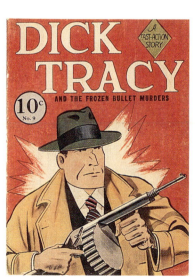

Dick Tracy and the
Frozen Bullet Murders
© 1936, 4" x 5½".
$40

A FAST-ACTION STORY
Dell

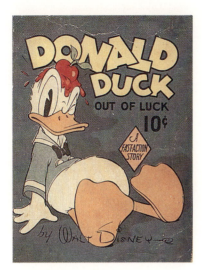

Donald Duck Out of Luck
© 1940, 4" x 5½".
$35

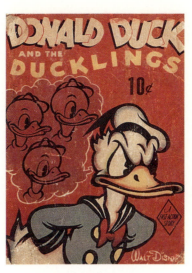

Donald Duck and the
Ducklings
© 1938, 4" x 5½".
$35

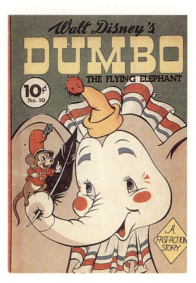

Dumbo The Flying Elephant
© 1941, 4" x 5½".
$55

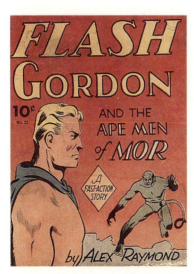

Flash Gordon and the
Ape Men of Mor
© 1942, 4" x 5½".
$50

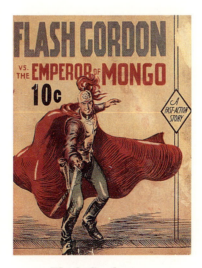

Flash Gordon vs.
The Emperor of Mongo
© 1936, 4" x 5½".
$85

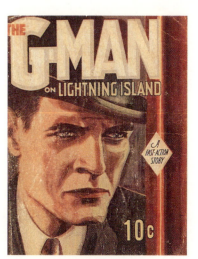

The G-Man on
Lightning Island
© 1936, 4" x 5½".
$35

A FAST-ACTION STORY
Dell

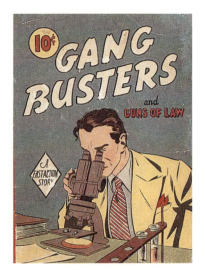

Gang Busters and
Guns of Law
© 1940, 4" x 5½".
$35

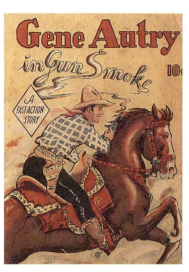

Gene Autry in Gun Smoke
© 1938, 4" x 5½".
$35

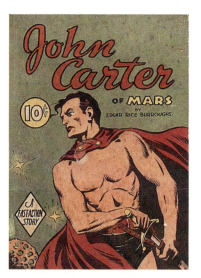

John Carter of Mars
© 1940, 4" x 5½".
$60

The Katzenjammer Kids
© 1942, 4" x 5½".
$40

Little Orphan Annie
Under The Big Top
© 1938, 4" x 5½".
$50

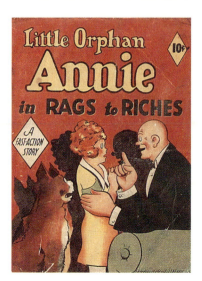

Little Orphan Annie in
Rags to Riches
© 1938, 4" x 5½".
$55

A FAST-ACTION STORY
Dell

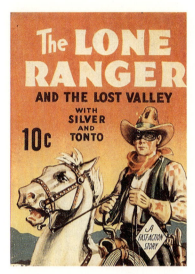

The Lone Ranger and the Lost
Valley with Silver and Tonto
© 1938, 4" x 5½".
$50

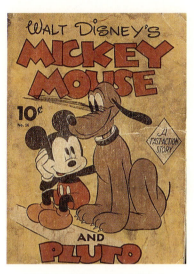

Mickey Mouse and Pluto
© 1938, 4" x 5½".
$50

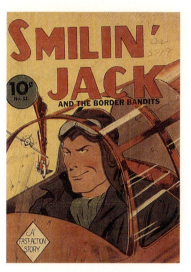

Smilin' Jack and the
Border Bandits
© 1941, 4" x 5½".
$20

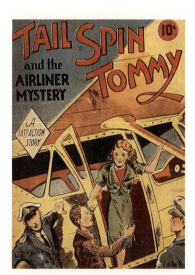

Tail Spin Tommy and the
Airliner Mystery
© 1938, 4" x 5½".
$25

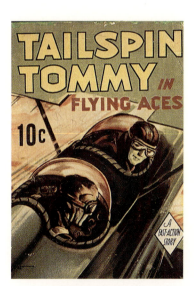

Tailspin Tommy in
Flying Aces
© 1938, 4" x 5½".
$25

Tarzan with the Tarzan
Twins in the Jungle
© 1938, 4" x 5½".
$35

75

A FAST-ACTION STORY
Dell

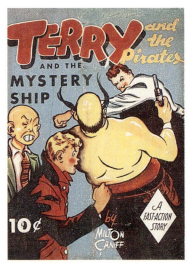

Terry and the Pirates
and the Mystery Ship
© 1938, 4" x 5½".
$20

Tom Mix Avenges The Dry
Gulched Range King
© 1939, 4" x 5½".
$25

Zane Grey's King of the
Royal Mounted Policing
the Frozen North
© 1938, 4" x 5½".
$25

Black Beauty
© 1934, book #1047,
4½" x 5".
$40

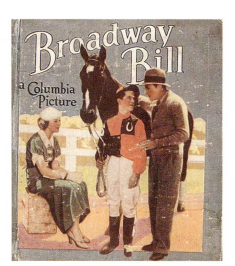

Broadway Bill
© 1935, book #1100,
4⅝" x 5⅛".
$15

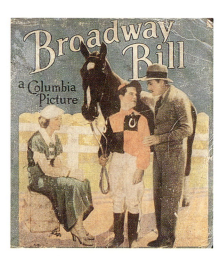

Broadway Bill
© 1935, book #1580,
paperback, 4½" x 5".
$15

Saalfield

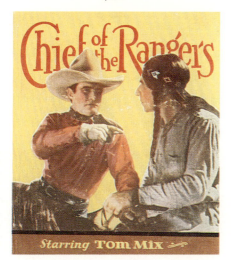

Burn 'em up Barnes
© 1935, book #1321, 4½" x 4¾".
$20

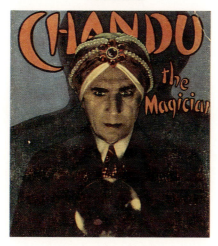

Chandu The Magician
© 1935, book #1323,
paperback, 4½" x 4¾".
$20

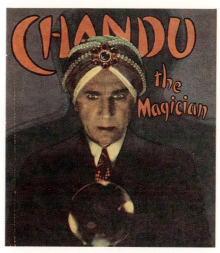

Chandu The Magician
© 1935, book #1093, 4½" x 5".
$20

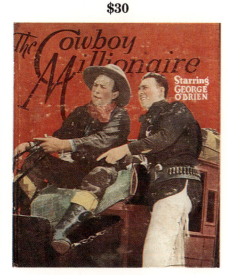

Chief of the Rangers Starring
Tom Mix, © 1935, book #1101,
4½" x 5".
$30

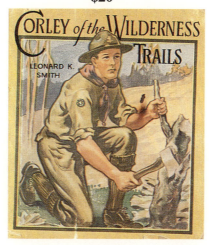

Corley of the Wilderness Trails
© 1937, book #1607, paperback,
4½" x 4¾".
$20

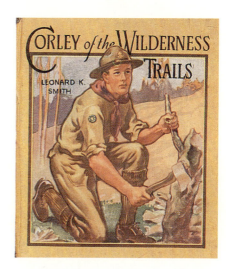

Corley of the Wilderness Trails
© 1937, book #1127, 4½" x 5".
$20

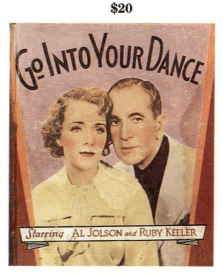

The Cowboy Millionaire
© 1935, book #1106, 4½" x 5".
$30

Go Into Your Dance
© 1935, book #109, 4½" x 5".
$20

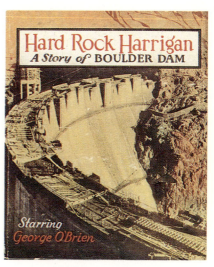

Hard Rock Harrigan
A Story of Boulder Dam
© 1935, book #1111, 4½" x 5".
$20

Saalfield

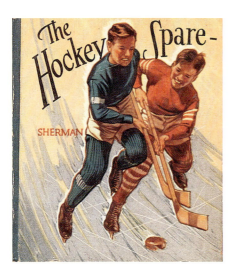
The Hockey Spare
© 1937, book #1125, 4½" x 5".
$25

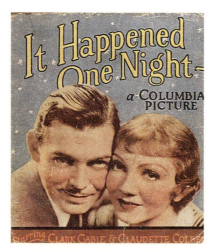
It Happened One Night,
© 1933 and 1935, book #1578,
paperback, 4½" x 4¾".
$25

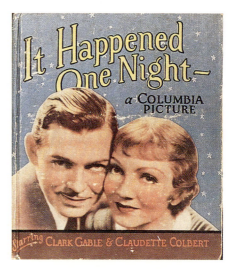
It Happened One Night
© 1933 and 1935,
book #1098, 4½" x 5".
$25

Just Kids and the
Mysterious Stranger,
© 1935, book #1324, 4½" x 5".
$20

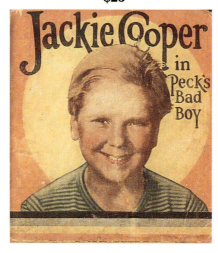
Jackie Cooper in Peck's Bad Boy,
© 1934, book #1314, 4½" x 4¾",
paperback. **$25**

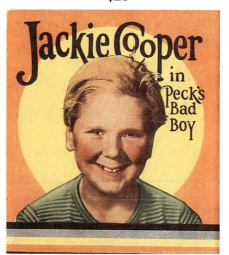
Jackie Cooper in Peck's Bad Boy,
© 1934, book #1084, 4½" x 5".
$30

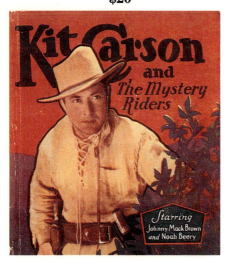
Kit Carson and The Mystery Riders
© 1935, book #1105, 4½" x 5".
$30

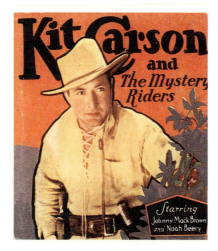
Kit Carson and The Mystery Riders
© 1935, book #1585,
4½" x 5", paperback.
$25

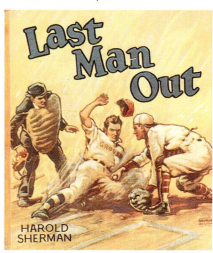
Last Man Out
© 1937, book #1128, 4½" x 5".
$20

Saalfield

Laurel and Hardy
© 1934, book #1086, 4½" x 5".
$40

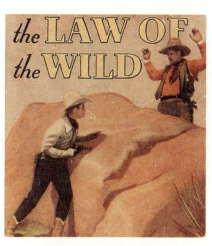

The Law of the Wild
© 1935, book #1322,
paperback, 4½" x 4¾".
$20

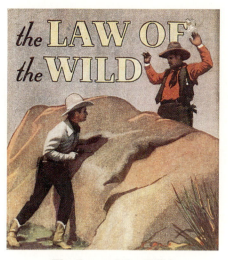

The Law of the Wild
© 1935, book #1092, 4½" x 5".
$25

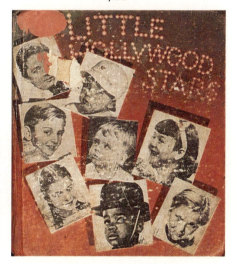

Little Hollywood Stars
© 1935, book #1112, 4½" x 5".
$35

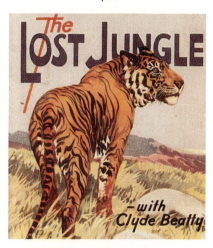

The Lost Jungle
© 1936, book #1583,
paperback, 4½" x 4¾".
$25

The Lost Jungle
© 1936, book #1103, 4½" x 5".
$30

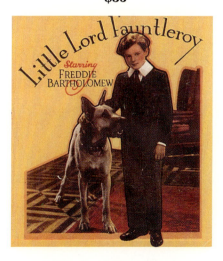

Little Lord Fauntleroy,
© 1936, book #1598, 4½" x 5".
$25

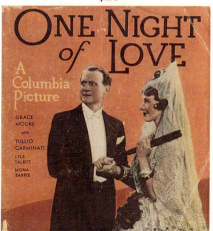

One Night of Love, © 1935, book
#1099, paperback, 4½" x 4¾".
$20

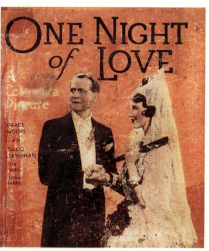

One Night of Love
© 1935, book #1579, 4½" x 5".
$25

Saalfield

Our Gang, © 1934, book #1085, paperback, 4½" x 4¾".
$30

Our Gang
© 1934, book #1315, 4½" x 5".
$35

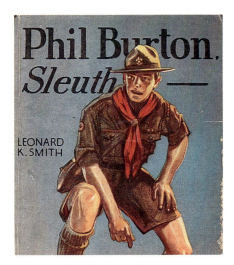

Phil Burton Sleuth
© 1937, book #1130, 4½" x 5".
$20

Popeye's Ark
© 1936, book #1117, 4½" x 5".
$35

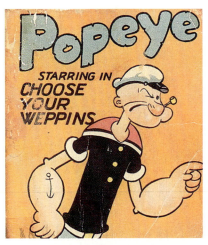

Popeye Starring in
Choose Your Weppins, © 1935
and 1936, book #1593, 4½" x 5".
$35

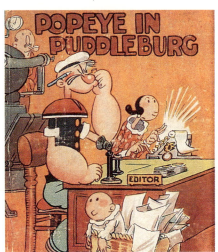

Popeye in Puddleburg,
© 1934, book #1088, 4½" x 5".
$45

Shirley Temple in The Little Colonel
© 1935, book #1895, 4½" x 5".
$30

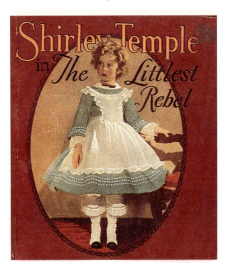

Shirley Temple in The Littlest Rebel
© 1935, book #1115, 4½" x 5".
$35

The Story of Shirley Temple
©1934, book #1319,
paperback, 4½" x 4¾"
$30

Saalfield

The Story of Shirley Temple,
© 1934, book #1089, 4½" x 5".
$35

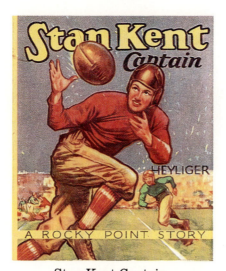

Stan Kent Captain,
© 1937, book #1132, 4½" x 5".
$25

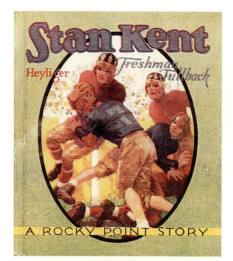

Stan Kent Freshman Fullback,
© 1936, book #1120, 4½" x 5".
$25

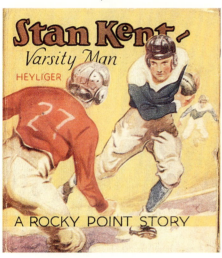

Stan Kent Varsity Man,
© 1936, book #1123, 4½" x 5".
$30

The Steel Arena
© 1936, book #1584, 4½" x 5".
$30

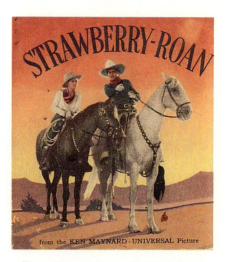

Strawberry-Roan, © 1934, book
#1320, paperback, 4½" x 4¾".
$35

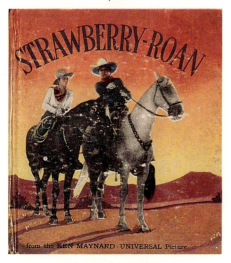

Strawberry-Roan,
© 1934, book #1090, 4½" x 5".
$40

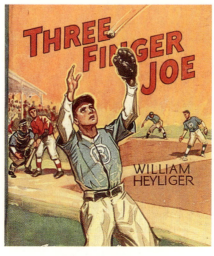

Three Finger Joe,
© 1937, book #1129, 4½" x 5".
$15

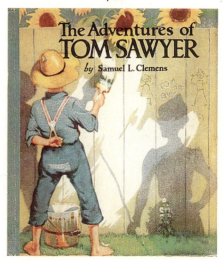

The Adventures of Tom Sawyer,
© 1934, book #1058, 4½" x 5".
$25

Saalfield

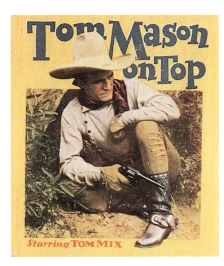

Tom Mason on Top,
© 1935, book #1102, 4½" x 5".
$30

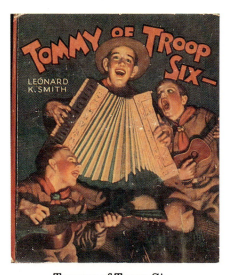

Tommy of Troop Six,
© 1937, book #1126, 4½" x 5".
$20

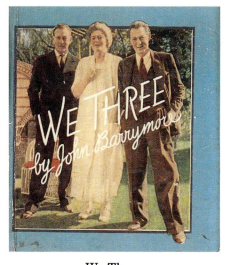

We Three,
© 1935, book #1109, 4½" x 5".
$25

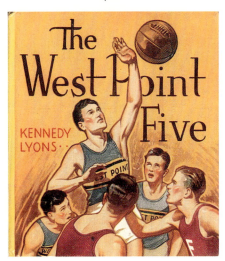

The West Point Five,
© 1937, book #1124, 4½" x 5".
$10

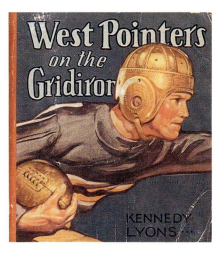

West Pointers on the Gridiron,
© 1936, book #1601, paperback,
4½" x 4¾". – **$20**

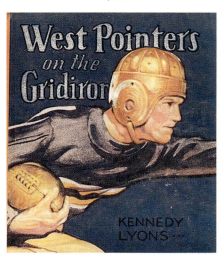

West Pointers on the Gridiron,
© 1936, book #1121, 4½" x 5".
$25

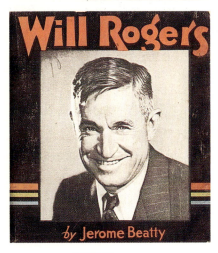

Will Rogers,
© 1935, book #1576, 4½" x 5".
$15

The Winged Four,
© 1937, book #1131, 4½" x 5".
$20

$1000 Reward, © 1938,
book # 1155, 3½" x 4½".
$20

Saalfield

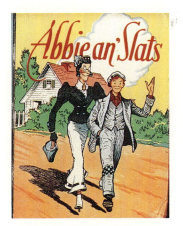
Abbie an' Slats, © 1940, book # 1175, 3½" x 4½".
$30

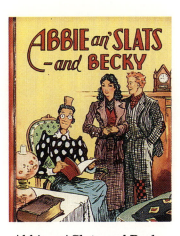
Abbie an' Slats and Becky, © 1940, book # 1182, 3½" x 4½".
$25

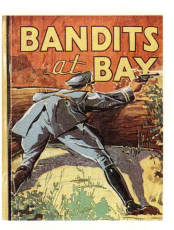
Bandits at Bay, © 1938, book #1138, 3½" x 4½".
$35

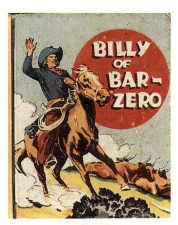
Billy of Bar Zero, © 1940, book # 1178, 3½" x 4½".
$25

Billy the Kid's Pledge, © 1940, book # 1174, 3½" x 4½".
$25

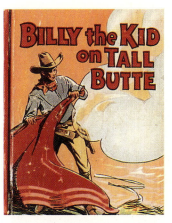
Billy the Kid on Tall Butte, © 1939, book # 1159, 3½" x 4½".
$30

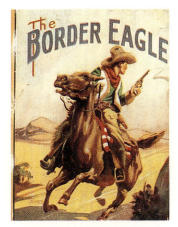
The Border Eagle, © 1938, book # 1139, 3½" x 4½".
$15

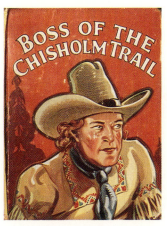
Boss of the Chisholm Trail, © 1939, book # 1153, 3½" x 4½".
$15

Broncho Bill, © 1940, book # 1181, 3½" x 4½".
$20

Saalfield

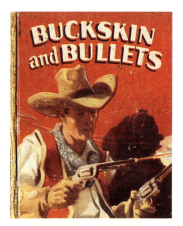

Buckskin and Bullets,
© 1938, book # 1135,
3½" x 4½".
$25

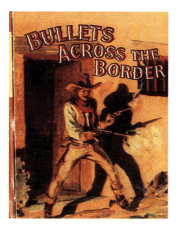

Bullets Across The Border,
© 1938, book # 1142,
3½" x 4½".
$25

Bullet Benton, © 1939,
book # 1169, 3½" x 4½".
$20

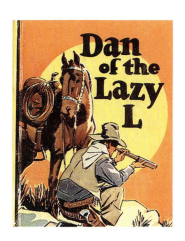

Dan of the Lazy L,
© 1939, book # 1160,
3½" x 4½".
$15

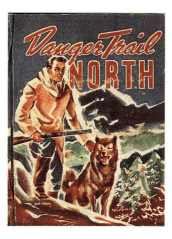

Danger Trail North,
© 1940, book # 1177,
3½" x 4½".
$20

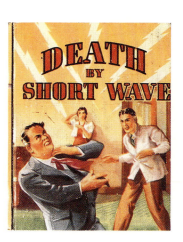

Death By Short Wave,
© 1938, book # 1151,
3½" x 4½".
$30

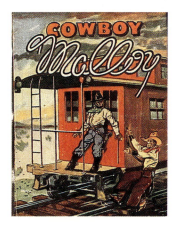

Cowboy Malloy,
© 1940, book # 1171,
3½" x 4½".
$25

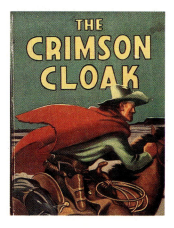

The Crimson Cloak,
© 1939, book # 1161,
3½" x 4½".
$20

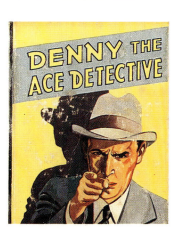

Denny The Ace Detective,
© 1938, book # 1156,
3½" x 4½".
$25

Saalfield

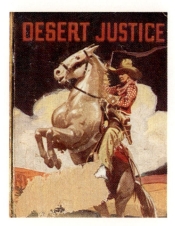

Desert Justice,
© 1938, book # 1136,
3½" x 4½".
$25

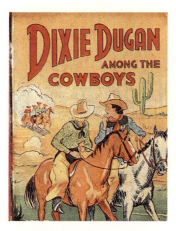

Dixie Dugan Among the
Cowboys, © 1939,
book # 1167, 3½" x 4½".
$35

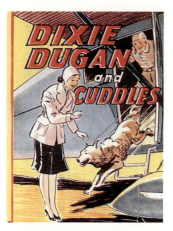

Dixie Dugan and Cuddles,
© 1940, book # 1188,
3½" x 4½".
$35

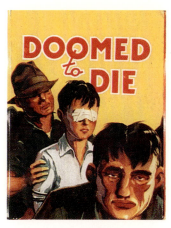

Doomed to Die,
© 1938, book # 1137,
3½" x 4½".
$15

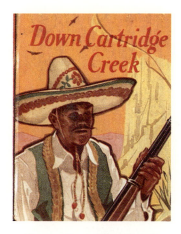

Down Cartridge Creek,
© 1938, book # 1140,
3½" x 4½".
$15

A G-Man in Action,
© 1940, book # 1173,
3½" x 4½".
$25

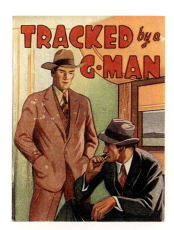

Tracked by a G-Man,
© 1939, book # 1158,
3½" x 4½".
$30

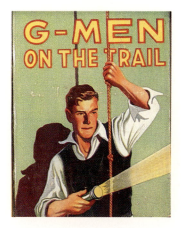

G-Men on the Trail,
© 1938, book # 1157,
3½" x 4½".
$35

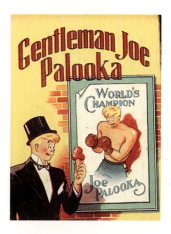

Gentleman Joe Palooka,
© 1940, book # 1176,
3½" x 4½".
$35

Saalfield

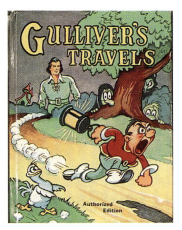
Gullivers Travels,
© 1939, book # 1172,
3½" x 4½".
$15

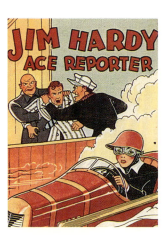
Jim Hardy Ace Reporter,
© 1940, book # 1180,
3½" x 4½".
$25

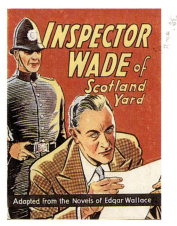
Inspector Wade
of Scotland Yard, © 1940,
book # 1186, 3½" x 4½".
$25

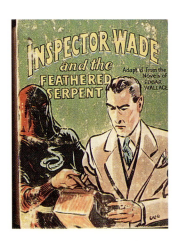
Inspector Wade and the
Feathered Serpent,
© 1940, book # 1194,
3½" x 4½".
$25

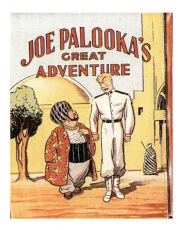
Joe Palooka's
Great Adventure,
© 1939, book # 1168,
3½" x 4½".
$30

Johnny Forty-Five,
© 1939, book # 1164,
3½" x 4½".
$30

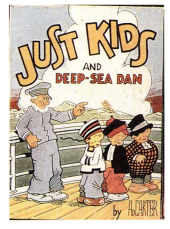
Just Kids and
Deep-Sea Dan, © 1940,
book # 1184, 3½" x 4½".
$20

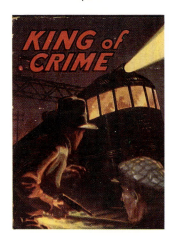
King of Crime,
© 1935, book # 1134,
3½" x 4½".
$20

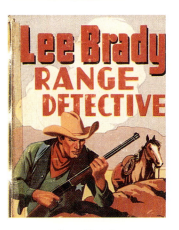
Lee Brady
Range Detective,
© 1938, book # 1149,
3½" x 4½".
$15

Saalfield

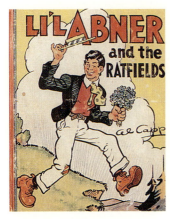

Li'L Abner and the Ratfields,
© 1940, book # 1193,
3½" x 4½".
$15

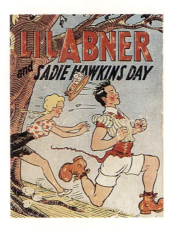

Li'L Abner and Sadie
Hawkins Day,
© 1940, book # 1193,
3½" x 4½".
$40

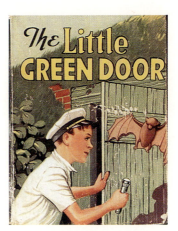

The Little Green Door,
© 1938, book # 1148,
3½" x 4½".
$15

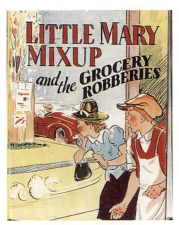

Little Mary Mixup and
the Grocery Robberies,
© 1940, book # 1192,
3½" x 4½".
$15

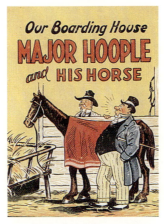

Our Boarding House Major
Hoople and His Horse,
© 1935 & 40, book # 1190,
3½" x 4½".
$25

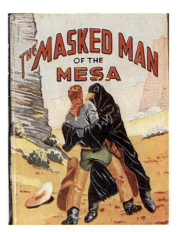

The Masked Man
of the Mesa,
© 1939, book # 1165,
3½" x 4½".
$15

Mickey Finn, © 1940,
book # 1170, 3½" x 4½".
$20

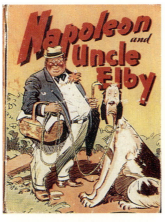

Napoleon and Uncle Elby,
© 1938, book # 1150,
3½" x 4½".
$20

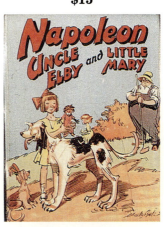

Napoleon, Uncle Elby
and Little Mary,
© 1939, book # 1166,
3½" x 4½".
$20

Saalfield

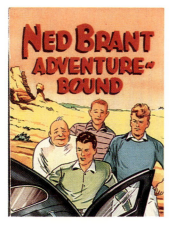

Ned Brant
Adventure-Bound,
© 1940, book # 1179,
3½" x 4½".
$15

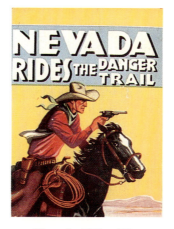

Nevada Rides The
Danger Trail, © 1938,
book # 1146, 3½" x 4½".
$20

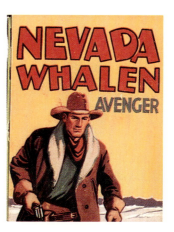

Nevada Whalen Avenger,
© 1938, book # 1147,
3½" x 4½".
$20

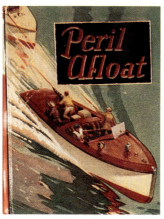

Peril Afloat,
© 1938, book # 1143,
3½" x 4½".
$15

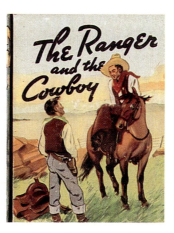

The Ranger and
the Cowboy,
© 1939, book # 1163,
3½" x 4½".
$15

Rangers on the
Rio Grande,
© 1938, book # 1154,
3½" x 4½".
$20

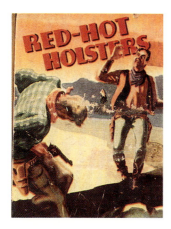

Red-Hot Holsters,
© 1938, book # 1145,
3½" x 4½".
$15

Secret Agent K-7,
© 1940, book # 1191,
3½" x 4½".
$15

Son of Mystery,
© 1939, book # 1152,
3½" x 4½".
$15

Saalfield

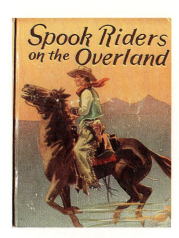 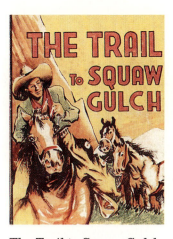 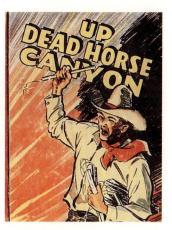

Spook Riders on the
Overland,
© 1938, book # 1144,
3½" x 4½".
$20

The Trail to Squaw Gulch,
© 1940, book # 1185,
3½" x 4½".
$15

Up Dead Horse Canyon,
© 1940, book # 1189,
3½" x 4½".
$15

Just Kids, © 1934, book #1052, 3½" x 8".
$15

Katzenjammer Kids in the Mountains,
© 1934, book #1055, 3½" x 8".
$25

Saalfield

Little Annie Rooney,
© 1934, book #1054, 3½" x 8".
$15

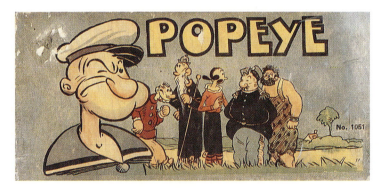

Popeye,
© 1934, book #1051, 3½" x 8".
$35

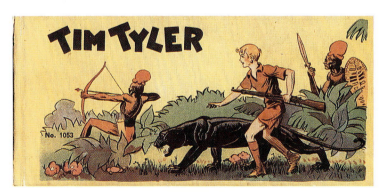

Tim Tyler,
© 1934, book #1053, 3½" x 8".
$20

Saalfield

Barney Google, © 1935,
book #1313, 2¼" x 2¾".
$30

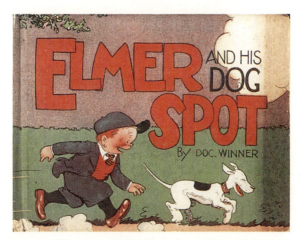

Elmer and His Dog Spot, © 1935,
book #1081, 2¼" x 3".
$15

Little Jimmy's Gold Hunt,
© 1935, book #1087, 2¼" x 3".
$15

The Adventures of Pete The Tramp,
© 1935, book #1082, 2¼" x 3".
$20

Saalfield

Polly and Her Pals
on the Farm, © 1934,
book #1310, 1 7/8" x 2 3/4".
$15

Brick Bradford in The City
Beneath The Sea ,
© 1934, book #1309,
paperback, 1 7/8" x 2 3/4".
$20

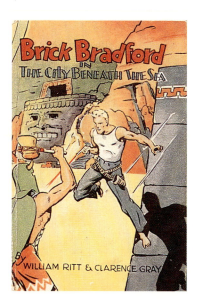

Brick Bradford in The City
Beneath The Sea, © 1934,
book #1059, 1 7/8" x 2 7/8".
$20

A LYNN BOOK

Chip Collins Adventures on Bat Island, © 1935, book #L14, 2¼" x 2⅞".
$15

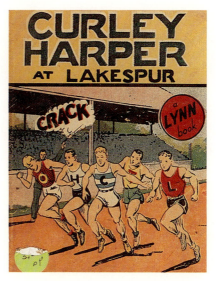

Curley Harper at Lakespur, © 1935, book #L19, 2¼" x 2⅞".
$15

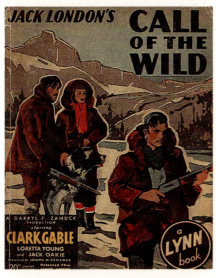

Jack London's Call of the Wild, © 1935, book #L11, 2¼" x 2⅞".
$20

Victor Hugo's Les Miserables, © 1935, book #L10, 2¼" x 2⅞".
$20

A LYNN BOOK

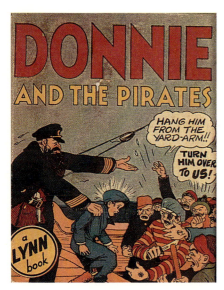

Donnie and the Pirates, © 1935, book #L13, 2¼" x 2⅞".
$15

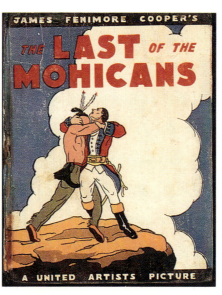

The Last of the Mohicans, © 1936, book #L30, 2¼" x 2⅞".
$30

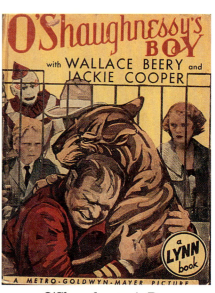

O'Shaughnessy's Boy, © 1935, book #L17, 2¼" x 2⅞".
$20

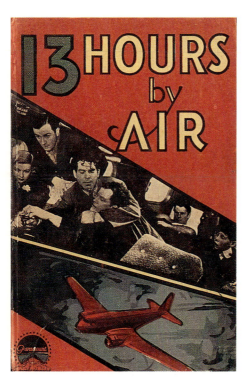

13 Hours by Air, © 1936, book #26, 5" x 7½".
$30

Ceiling Zero, © 1936, 5" x 7½".
$35

A LYNN BOOK

Dumb Dora & Bing Brown,
© 1936, 5" x 7½".
$20

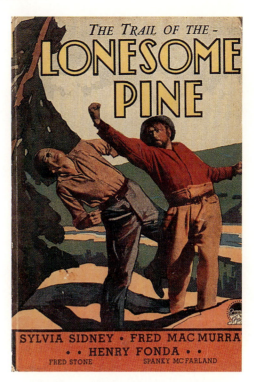

The Trail of the Lonesome Pine,
© 1936, book #25, 5" x 7½".
$40

ENGLE VAN-WISEMAN
Five Star Library

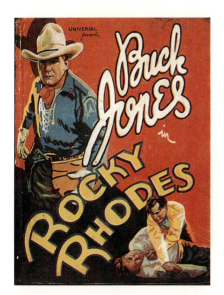

Buck Jones in Rocky Rhodes,
© 1935, 4¼" x 5⅝".
$15

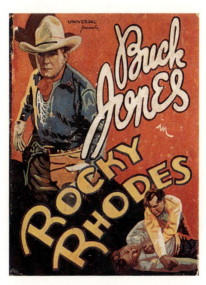

Buck Jones in Rocky Rhodes,
© 1935, book #20, 4¼" x 5⅝".
$15

The Count of Monte Cristo,
© 1934, book #1, 4¼" x 5⅝".
$20

ENGLE VAN-WISEMAN
Five Star Library

The Count of Monte Cristo,
© 1934, book #1, 4¼" x 5⅝".
$20

The Fighting President,
© 1934, book #6, 4¼" x 5⅝".
$15

Frankie Thomas in
A Dog of Flanders
© 1935, book #16, 4¼" x 5⅝".
$15

Jackie Cooper in Dinky,
© 1935, book #13, 4¼" x 5⅝".
$20

Great Expectations,
© 1934, book #8, 4¼" x 5⅝".
$15

Buck Jones in The Red Rider,
© 1934, book #3, 4¼" x 5⅝".
$15

ENGLE VAN-WISEMAN
Five Star Library

The Little Minister,
© 1935, book #9, 4¼" x 5⅝".
$20

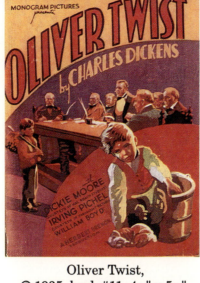

Oliver Twist,
© 1935, book #11, 4¼" x 5⅝".
$15

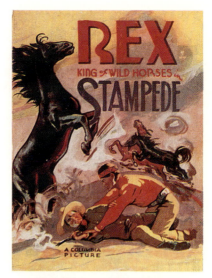

Rex King of Wild Horses
in Stampede
© 1935, book #12, 4¼" x 5⅝".
$15

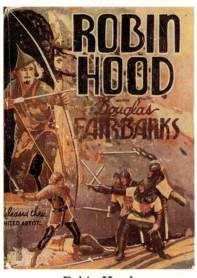

Robin Hood,
© 1935, book #10, 4¼" x 5⅝".
$15

Tim McCoy Speedwings,
© 1935, book #14, 4¼" x 5⅝".
$15

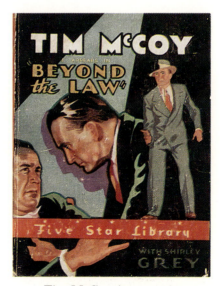

Tim McCoy Appears in
"Beyond The Law",
© 1934, book #2, 4¼" x 5⅝".
$15

Wheels of Destiny,
© 1934, book #5, 4¼" x 5⅝".
$15

FAMOUS COMICS
(Three Book Set with Box No. 684)

Box to the original set

King Feature's Syndicate, © 1934.
$65 for box set

THE WORLD SYNDICATE PUBLISHING CO.
By J. Carroll Mansfield

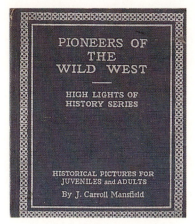

Pioneers of The Wild West,
© 1933, 2" x 4½".
$10

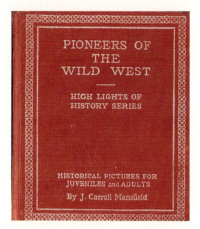

Pioneers of The Wild West,
© 1933, 2" x 4½".
$10

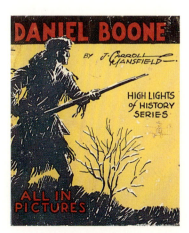

Daniel Boone,
© 1934, 2" x 4½".
$10

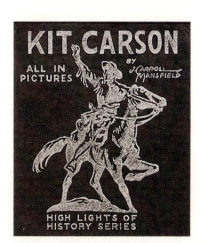

Kit Carson,
© 1933, 2" x 4½".
$10

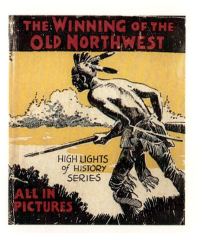

The Winning of the
Old Northwest,
© 1934, 2" x 4½".
$10

SAMUEL LOWE CO., KENOSHA, WISCONSIN
© James and Johnathan Co. – Ten Cowboy Stories

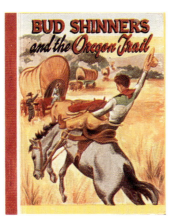

Bud Shinners and the
Oregon Trail,
© 1949, 3½" x 4¼".
$5

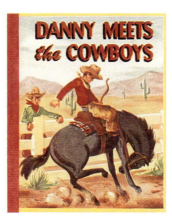

Danny Meets the Cowboys,
© 1949, 3½" x 4¼".
$5

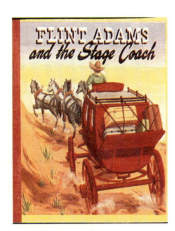

Flint Adams and the
Stage Coach,
© 1949, 3½" x 4¼".
$5

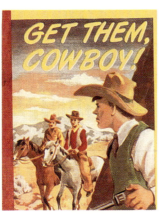

Get Them, Cowboy!
© 1949, 3½" x 4¼".
$5

Little Tex Comes
to XY Ranch,
© 1949, 3½" x 4¼".
$5

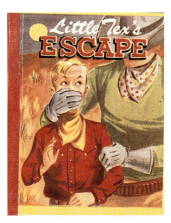

Little Tex's Escape,
© 1949, 3½" x 4¼".
$5

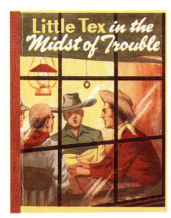

Little Tex in the
Midst of Trouble,
© 1949, 3½" x 4¼".
$5

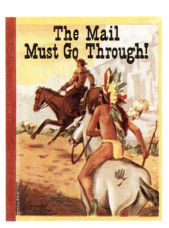

The Mail Must Go
Through!
© 1949, 3½" x 4¼".
$5

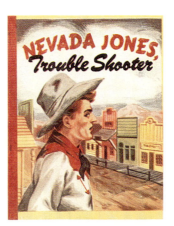

Nevada Jones, Trouble
Shooter,
© 1949, 3½" x 4¼".
$5

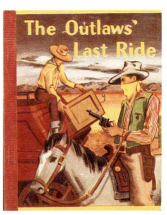

The Outlaws' Last Ride,
© 1949, 3½" x 4¼".
$5

GOLDEN PRESS, NY

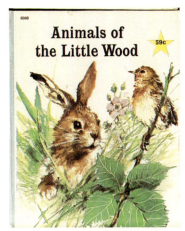

Animals of the
Little Wood, © 1967,
Western Publishing Co.,
Inc., book #6080, 3⅝" x 4⅝".
$5

Autumn Tales, © 1955,
Western Publishing Co.,
Inc., book #6024, 3⅝" x 4⅝".
$5

Winter Tales, © 1955,
Western Publishing Co.,
Inc., book #6079, 3⅝" x 4⅝".
$5

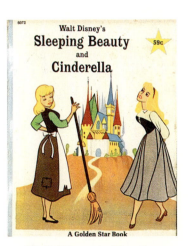

Walt Disney's Sleeping
Beauty and Cinderella,
© 1967, book #6072,
3⅝" x 4⅝".
$10

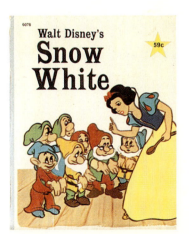

Walt Disney's Snow White,
© 1967, book #6076,
3⅝" x 4⅝".
$10

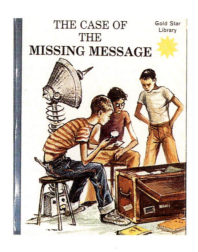

The Case of the Missing Message, © 1966, the text is by Gold Pleasure Books, printed in Italy, Golden Pleasure Books, London, 3 5/8" x 4 5/8".
$5

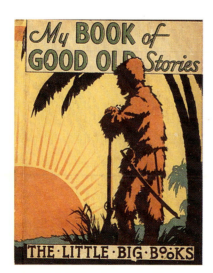

My Book of Good Old Stories, © 1928, McLaughlin Bros., Inc., Springfield, Mass., marked The Little Big Books (new matter printed 1934), book #1828, 4" x 5 3/8".
$10

Nature Stories for Tiny Folk, © 1928, McLaughlin Bros., Inc., Springfield, Mass., marked The Little Big Books (new matter printed 1934), book #2215, 4" x 5 3/8".
$10